Frankie looked up into his face, which was broodingly handsome in the dark shadows, and smelled the warmth of his skin, and a sudden, overwhelming desire for him arrowed through her. She closed her eyes against the assault on her senses. Was she crazy? She'd never felt like this before, not for any man, but the feeling was unmistakable. She wanted Cal; she wanted him as her lover, and she wanted him with a brute and primitive longing that almost propelled her hard into his arms.

She opened her eyes again, reeling inside from her feelings, and met Cal's steady gaze.

'What's the matter?' His voice was roughened. 'There's no danger.'

'I know,' she lied. But there was. The danger was here in the tent, beside her, inside her. And it was far more dangerous, far more wild, than any wild animal.

AFRICAN ASSIGNMENT

BY

CAROL GREGOR

MILLS & BOON LIMITED
ETON HOUSE   18–24 PARADISE ROAD
RICHMOND   SURREY   TW9 1SR

*First published in Great Britain 1991
by Mills & Boon Limited*

© Carol Gregor 1991

*Australian copyright 1991
Philippine copyright 1991
This edition 1991*

ISBN 0 263 77301 9·

*Set in 10 on 12 pt Linotron Times
01-9111-51419
Typeset in Great Britain by Centracet, Cambridge
Made and printed in Great Britain*

CHAPTER ONE

IT WAS five to three. Frankie turned the corner and checked the address. Number five. This was it, this imposing, colonnaded Regency house, with its marble steps and gleaming white stucco, and the number painted black in a round, raised panel on one of the pillars.

She swallowed, intimidated by the austere grandness of the entrance, and ran her hands nervously down the sides of her dress. The beige cotton shirt-waister felt strange to her touch, and she grimaced. The dress turned her into an impostor. It was too neat, too anonymous. She hated it. What she usually wore were tight leggings with T-shirts, or swirling dresses in brightly coloured Indian cottons, but Aunt Jenny had insisted that she needed a sensible outfit for occasions such as these, and today she had to acknowledge that her aunt had been right. None of her other clothes would have been suitable for an interview for a mystery job with an entirely unknown boss.

She looked up. The windows of the house looked cold and blank and there was not so much as an empty milk bottle on the step to show signs of human habitation.

Well, it didn't matter, she told herself with forced bravado. If she didn't like the sound of the job, or didn't like the look of Mr Fenton, then she needn't have anything to do with it. And she probably wouldn't. She certainly didn't like the abrupt way she had been summoned to see him. She pushed the bell, tipped her chin defiantly, and waited.

Somewhere in the dim recesses of the house there was a mournful chime. She waited. The carrier-bag she was carrying was so heavy that it cut her hand. She shifted it to the other hand. Her flimsy courage was ebbing with every minute. For two pins she would turn and flee, but she knew she couldn't. She had to give it a try—after all, what other hope did she have of landing a job? And without a job she was penniless, unable to pay the rent and forced to flee in disgrace back home to Yorkshire.

She pushed the bell again and this time footsteps responded to its dismal tone. A middle-aged woman opened the door.

'Yes?' Her tone was frosty.

'I'm Frankie. Frankie O'Shea.'

'Oh.' The woman's thin eyebrows rose in blatant astonishment.

'You *were* expecting me?' Frankie's stretched nerves jangled. Maybe she'd got the wrong day, and blown her chance of this job before she'd even started?

'Yes, yes. It's just that—oh, well, never mind. You'd better come in, anyway.' She held the door open for her to walk in. The hall was huge and cavernous. The woman briskly led the way through to a large drawing-room.

'I'm Elaine Pye, Mr Fenton's secretary. Would you mind waiting here? I'm afraid he got delayed in Paris this morning. He's somewhere between Heathrow and here. He should have been here by now, but you know what the traffic can be like.'

'Er—yes.' She longed to ask Elaine Pye who Cal Fenton was, and what he did—but the questions seemed foolish, and she was overawed by the cool distance of the woman's manner, and even more so by her surroundings.

She turned to take them in. Three floor-to-ceiling windows gave a superb view of the park. They were hung and draped with expensive navy silk hangings. The walls were palest grey with a faint silky sheen. Some obviously expensive but rather gloomy Dutch water-colours were hung here and there, and the mirror above the marble fireplace was gilded. There were two sofas, covered in grey striped fabric, but they looked stiff and cold, as if no one had ever used them to sit and talk and laugh.

She'd like to let Aunt Jenny loose in here, she thought, looking around. She'd light logs in the grate, and put a bowl of roses on the table. She'd open the windows to let a fresh breeze stir those sombre hangings, and add a few family photographs for warmth and clutter.

'Is this——' She turned to ask a question of Elaine Pye, but found that the woman had already stepped silently away, leaving her alone.

She went instinctively to the window. There were children playing on the grass of the park, but the windows were double-glazed and no sound of their laughter penetrated through to her.

'Oh, lord,' she muttered, and set down her carrier-bag on the floor to ease her hand. As she did so a black taxi cruised to a halt in the street below. A dark-haired man unfolded himself and stepped hastily up the steps. She heard a key in the door, then a slam.

'Elaine!' The shout was deep and peremptory. She heard high heels tapping on the marble floor in answer to the summons. 'What time am I supposed to be in Brighton?'

'Six o'clock. The judges are meeting for drinks first.'

'Hell's teeth! Next time one of these damn award things comes up, remind me to have nothing to do with it.'

'Frankie O'Shea's in the drawing-room.'

'Who? Oh, yes. Right. I'll get that over with first. I'll only be a minute. Get me Andy Rawlins in New York, will you?'

Get her over with? Frankie bridled.

'Yes. Cal, before you go in, I think you should know——'

'I'm busy. Tell me later.'

She heard impatient steps striding towards the room where she stood, and suddenly her heart dipped with a premonition of disaster. She was in a condemned cell, she thought, with the executioner coming to get her, and there was not a thing she could do about it. She was rooted to the spot. She swallowed fast several times as the door opened.

She saw a tall man come in, a man dressed in black— black shirt, black leather jacket, black trousers. He had black hair, and a black travelling-bag which he threw carelessly on to a chair, and his look was black with impatience and fatigue.

'Frankie? I'm sorry you've had to wait.'

She moved forward, away from the shadows of the curtain where she had been standing. Her dress was pale in the gloomy room, and her auburn hair gleamed lustrously in the sunlight that slanted through the window.

She smiled and held out her hand, but his face was aghast.

'My God!' he said. 'You're a girl!'

His words echoed around the room, making her head reel. Then her thoughts snapped into focus.

'Of course I'm a girl! What did you expect?'

'What do you think I expected? A boy. A young man. What sort of name is Frankie for a girl?'

'A perfectly good one. It's short for Francesca, which I've always hated. The nuns tried to make me use it, but I refused. I *feel* like a Frankie.'

'Nuns?'

'At the convent.'

'A convent girl! This gets worse and worse. Well, it would have been nice if someone had bothered to tell me! All I was told was that Mike O'Shea's brat was looking for something to do. Then I was given your name.'

'Brat!'

He dashed an impatient hand through his hair. 'Well, they might have said child, or offspring, or something. I don't remember exactly. I can tell you one thing— they certainly didn't say daughter, or you wouldn't be standing here today. Hell and damnation! What am I going to do now?'

Anger robbed her of all her shyness. She marched forward, round the end of a sofa, towards him. 'It's wasted my time, too! This whole thing is ridiculous. If you'd had the basic courtesy to ring me, and explain what you were looking for, this would never have happened! All I got was that brusque little note giving me the time and place.'

His look was unbending. 'There's been no time for niceties like telephone calls. It's just been crazy lately. I had a lad all lined up to come with me, but he suddenly decided he'd rather crew a yacht round the Mediterranean for the summer. I thought any boy of Mike O'Shea's would be ideal, so I grabbed the chance.'

His words stopped her in her tracks. 'You mean you actually knew my father? Not just by reputation?' She was near him now, and as she spoke she looked fully into his face for the first time.

'Oh!'

What she saw there made her gasp. She felt as if the breath had been literally knocked out of her. Cal Fenton was tall and athletic, younger than his dark figure had first appeared. He had black hair, straight black eyebrows and a cuttingly straight mouth, but it was his eyes that took the air from her body. They were grey and handsome, but they were also the bleakest eyes she had ever seen in her life. When she looked into them she saw cold winter days when the sky was low and the rain sheeted down and there seemed to be no hope or happiness left anywhere in the world.

'What's the matter?' he snapped. 'You're looking as if you've seen a ghost.'

She shook her head. 'Nothing.' But that was exactly how she felt. As if she had seen a ghost—the ghost of lost joy and laughter. 'Did you really know my father?'

'Yes. I met him in the Middle East, years ago.' His voice was terse.

'Oh, I see! You're a foreign correspondent, like he was.'

He gave her a strange look. 'No. Photographer. Although it doesn't make much difference when you're all trying to survive in a war zone together.'

Her mouth turned down. 'Mike wasn't very good at surviving in the end though, was he?' There was still a raw pain in her words, despite the seven long years since the phone had rung at home in Yorkshire and shattered her childhood world forever.

His eyes went over her intently, then flicked away. 'It was a random car bomb,' he rapped out. 'It was just bad luck that he happened to be walking down that road when it happened.'

'Bad luck,' she said bitterly. 'Hardly. He'd chosen to be in Beirut. Bombs go off there all the time.'

'It was his job—a job he loved and was superb at.'

She turned away. The cold grey eyes were turned on her and she felt chilled by their light.

'I'm very sorry you lost your father,' he said, formally. 'It must have been hard for you and your mother——'

'My mother didn't know a thing about it! She was killed in a car accident when I was ten. We seem to be an extraordinarily unlucky family. Or maybe we're just careless!' To her utter horror she felt her voice go shaky with tears and she swallowed hard once or twice. Self-pity was not something she normally indulged in, but today wasn't turning out to be a normal sort of day at all.

'Well, I'm sorry,' he said behind her. 'But you had a fine father. One to be proud of. Now, though, if you'll excuse me, I've got a million things to do. I hope I haven't wasted too much of your afternoon.'

She whirled back to the present and turned to face him.

'Just as a matter of interest, what was this job anyway? What was so taxing about it that a girl couldn't possibly be considered capable of doing it?'

He looked at her and shrugged one shoulder carelessly. 'I'm convalescent, hurt this shoulder on my last assignment. I need someone to do my driving.'

'I can drive!'

'It's not only that. I'm flying to Africa for a few weeks. There's a job I have to do out there for a wildlife charity. They haven't got much money so I have to keep costs to a minimum. One tent, one hotel-room, all that——'

But she was scarcely listening. Africa! Flying to Africa! The words rang in her brain like a bell, and immediately a thousand images came tumbling through her mind. She saw golden plains, lions, wildebeest. She heard drums, and felt the hot sun on her face, and smelled the scent of dust and freedom, and suddenly, from nowhere, she knew that she wanted to go to Africa more than she had ever wanted anything in her life! She felt almost breathless with desire. So this was what she had been wanting, she thought with astonishment, remembering how bored and claustrophobic she had felt in her previous jobs. To travel the world, and find its wonders. Why had she never realised that before?

'Well, that's ridiculous,' she butted in bluntly, shouldering aside his words. 'There's no good reason why a girl couldn't do all that!'

'Have you even been listening to me?'

'Of course I have, but you're talking nonsense. Complete nonsense. Why, you might even do better taking a girl along! She could cook and—and——'

'And?' he said drily, and a spark flickered briefly in the coldness of his cutting gaze. 'You needn't go on. I've an active enough imagination—and that's another very good reason for not wanting mixed company. As far as I'm concerned, women are strictly an after-hours occupation. I can well do without those sorts of distractions when I'm trying to work.' He turned and picked up his bag. 'Don't bother to go on. You're not going to persuade me. My mind's made up.'

'Why, that's ridiculous! Women are people, not an "occupation"!'

'So I've been told.'

'Times have changed!'

'Some things never change.'

'Or some men!'

'That's as may be. But I don't intend to stand here wasting even more of my valuable time arguing gender politics. I think you know your way out.'

'I'll be glad to go!' The man was insufferable. She marched towards the door. Then something—maybe all the clamouring images of Africa that still rang in her head—made her pause and turn.

'When do you go?'

'On Friday.'

'You'll never find anyone else by then.'

'I'm sure I will.'

'What if you don't?'

'I'll manage alone.'

'You'll do no such thing.'

A voice from the hallway startled them both. Elaine Pye stood there, hands on her hips. She looked towards Frankie. 'He took a direct hit in that shoulder. Half the bones were shattered to pieces. The sling's only just come off and now he's talking about driving around the back of beyond on his own——'

'Elaine, don't nanny me or I'll fire you. Have you got Andy on line?'

'He's waiting now.'

'Then I'll say goodbye, Miss O'Shea. Elaine will show you out.' And he turned and was gone.

'Where was he shot?' she asked Elaine.

'Haiti. The election riots.'

'Oh,' she said, then her hands flew to her mouth. 'Oh! Of course! I've just realised! He's Cal Fenton, *the* Cal Fenton!'

Suddenly it all slotted into place. How he had known Mike, the bullet wound, the curt manner. Above all the bleak grey eyes. How could you look anything but bleak when you had had a ringside view of every war and famine and natural disaster the earth had managed to produce over the last ten years, and your pictures had become the world's best-known symbols of the hopelessness of modern times?

'I wasn't thinking—I didn't realise who he was——'

'I presume that makes two of you,' Elaine Pye said tartly. 'I'm sure he thought you were a boy. I would have warned him if there had been time.'

'He did.' She tossed her head, and raised her chin defiantly. 'I was a great disappointment to him—and that made two of us. I can assure you I have far better things to do with my time than to make fruitless trips across London.' And she brushed past the older woman and tapped down the steps without a backward glance.

CHAPTER TWO

'How was it?' Frankie's flatmate Alice asked, when she arrived back.

'Nice job, awful man. How was your day off?'

'Lovely. I slept all morning, then I went shopping.'

'Ugh. Before I do anything else, I'm going to take this dress off and put some of my real clothes on.'

'It is pretty ghastly,' Alice agreed readily. 'Why did you buy it?'

'I didn't. Aunt Jenny did, last year. She thinks it's just the thing for an interview and I didn't have the heart to disappoint her.'

Alice waited for her to reappear. She eyed Frankie's flounced mini-skirt and cropped top. 'That's much better,' she pronounced. 'Why was he awful, the man?'

'He was Cal Fenton.'

Alice's eyes widened. 'You mean the news photographer? But he's divine!' She shivered. 'He sort of smoulders out of his picture. You can see how he gets all his women.'

'What women?'

'Oh, he's always in the gossip columns with different ones; he's known for it. There was an article in the *Sunday Dispatch* recently.' Her hand described a banner headline in the air. '"HE LOVES—THEN HE LEAVES" That's what it said.'

'You don't want to believe all you read in that rag. Anyway, he doesn't smoulder in real life. He glowers.

15

And he isn't at all divine. He's very good-looking, but he's so cold and hard—and probably mean with it.'

'Starvation wages?'

'I don't know about that. We didn't get that far. I lacked one vital attribute for the job.'

'What was that?'

She paused, then giggled. 'He wanted a man.'

'Oh. That attribute.' Alice giggled with her. 'I wonder what he wanted it for?'

'I don't know. He's got a gammy shoulder and said he needed someone to do his driving, but I think he really just prefers the idea of a male lackey. Perhaps he feels he would have to be polite to a girl!'

'You don't think that deep down he's——' Alice paused delicately.

'Oh, no. No way!' She remembered the spark that had briefly warmed the depth of his grey gaze. 'On the contrary, he seems to believe women were put on this earth strictly for his leisure and pleasure.'

'What was the job?'

She sighed and turned wistful green eyes on her flatmate. 'Oh, Alice, it sounded wonderful. Fabulous. He was going to Africa to photograph animals. It would have meant going off camping in the bush——' She stared, unseeing, at the opposite wall. 'I would have loved to have gone. Even with Mr Gloom. . .'

'Couldn't you have persuaded him? Demonstrated your muscles?'

'No. His mind was made up the minute he saw me. He could barely give me the time of day.' She sighed heavily. 'Now what am I going to do?'

'Get another job.'

'Oh, yes. How?' Her eyes flashed. 'I've got no

references, remember. And what do I say when they ask me why I left my last job?'

'Tell them the truth. That your boss pawed and harassed you until you couldn't stand it another minute.'

She shuddered, remembering her miserable months at the West End advertising agency that she had walked out of last week. She had left Yorkshire and Aunt Jenny with such high hopes of making a new life in London, but it had all gone terribly wrong. She hated being a secretary, and hated even more having to fend off the hot-breathed attentions of a boss who clearly believed that when a girl said 'no' she really meant 'yes.'

'They wouldn't believe me.'

'Yes, they would, easily,' said Alice, crisply, her eyes going over her friend's tumble of auburn curls, her sparkling green eyes and dazzling smile. 'You've got to toughen up if you want to make it in the city.'

'I don't want to toughen up! I'm not sure I even want to make it in the city! I hate sitting behind a keyboard all day. It makes me feel so claustrophobic.'

'Well, what do you want to do?' Alice was clearly getting exasperated.

'I want to go to Africa!' Frankie lay back on the sofa and shut her eyes. The feeling was like a tempest inside her, a storm of longing unlocked by the uncaring Cal Fenton.

'With that insufferable man?'

'He'd be a small price to pay.'

'You've just run away from one arrogant male boss, remember.'

'I can't imagine Cal Fenton lunging for a quick

fumble by the coffee machine.' No, she thought, he'd click his fingers and expect any woman to come running.

Alice was blunt. 'Well, he obviously isn't going to employ you, so you might as well forget it. And, meanwhile, I hate to remind you of real life, but there's the rent to pay by Thursday.'

Frankie woke up late the next morning and knew from the silence that Alice had already left for work. She showered quickly and pulled on the same clothes she had worn the night before. Then, because it was a hot day, she brushed her hair up into a casual topknot and slipped on a pair of Indian sandals. The sensible dress and shoes she had worn yesterday were bundled unceremoniously together and thrust to the back of her wardrobe.

Then she made herself a coffee and sat at the kitchen table frowning, trying to work out how she had landed up in the mess she was in now.

Of course she had never really wanted to be a secretary. Back home in Yorkshire she had always preferred to be out in the fresh air, helping on the local farms. But Aunt Jenny, in her quietly insistent way, had outlined all the advantages of a diploma in office skills, and, in deference to her guardian, whom, she knew, had had to put up with so much from the wayward orphan landed in her charge, she had meekly taken the required college courses.

For a time she'd worked in a legal office in Skipton, but the sleepy local town had soon made her restless and she had thought that London would ease the cramped, stifling feeling inside her.

Yet it hadn't worked out like that. She'd made new

friends, particularly Alice, and had enjoyed living in her own flat, but typing in London had been just like typing in Skipton, with added complications, and two months after coming here she had had to ring her aunt and confess that she had just walked out of her first job in the middle of the week with neither her wages nor a reference.

Dear Aunt Jenny had uttered no word of criticism, but had simply sent her an emergency cheque and a brief letter saying she quite understood why she left, and that quite by chance she's just heard, through a former colleague of her father's, of a temporary job that might tide her over the next few weeks. And then had come the terse summons to see Cal Fenton.

Frankie sighed. Her aunt, bless her, had tried her best, and she was glad she had decided to make a surprise visit home to Yorkshire for her birthday this weekend. She looked forward to seeing her face when she handed over the crystal rose-bowl she had been saving up for ever since she had come down to London.

The rose-bowl.

She had bought it yesterday on her way to Cal Fenton's house, since her route had taken her right past the front door of Harrods. She could remember the way the heavy bag had cut into her hand. She turned this way, then that, but she knew as soon as she thought about it that she had not brought it back to the flat with her. It must still be sitting where she had left it, on the carpet in Cal Fenton's coldly opulent front room.

'Hell and damnation!' The phrase rose from somewhere to her lips. The last thing in the world she wanted to do was to trek back to that gloomy house, but the bowl had cost fifty pounds and there was no way she could afford to replace it.

She hesitated, eyeing the phone. Perhaps Elaine Pye would send it on for her, if she explained where she had left it. But then she would have to arrive in Yorkshire empty-handed. And although her own heart felt heavy with disappointment, she had looked forward to the pleasure that she knew would light up her aunt's face when the latter unwrapped her present and held the exquisite cut glass up to the light.

So it was with bitter determination that she again found herself ringing the bell of Cal Fenton's house. A woman who was hoovering the stairs opened the door immediately. 'They're in there.' She nodded her head towards the drawing-room and bent back to her work. Frankie marched towards the door, then hesitated.

Cal leaned with one elbow on the mantelpiece. She could see his look in the mirror and it was angry and dark. Elaine Pye stood in front of him, her legs planted stubbornly.'

'I don't care, Cal,' she was saying. 'You either have that cholera injection renewed, or I leave.'

'God dammit, I've told you. There's no time. I've got to be at the *Sunday Globe* all tomorrow, then I've got that North Sea trip on Thursday.'

'This afternoon, then.'

'You know I've got to get those Malaysian prints processed. I haven't got time to go running off to the doctor's.'

'Then I'll resign.'

He eyed her blackly. Neither of them noticed Frankie's slight figure in the doorway.

'Well, all right. I'll do a deal. If you get someone

round here this afternoon, I'll stop work long enough to let him stick his poisonous dart in me. Although I must be immune to just about everything by now. And why you persist in believing those things work, I'll never know.'

'I know that cholera's about the only thing you haven't had—and that could just be because I've made you keep your injections up.'

He sighed and put a hand up to his damaged shoulder, easing it. 'What on earth am I going to do about finding an assistant, Elaine? Those lads the agency sent round were hopeless.'

'I've told you. Your problem's not finding an assistant, it's finding one by Friday. Can't you delay your flight?'

He shook his head. 'London's stifling me. Anyway, I've got to get on with that wildlife job. I'm supposed to be in Iraq next month.'

'Can't you borrow someone from one of the newspapers?'

He shook his head. 'They're run on a shoestring. They haven't got staff to spare.'

'Find someone out there? Someone local?'

'I may have to. God knows who.' He thumped his fist on the marble mantelpiece. 'Why the hell couldn't Mike O'Shea have fathered a son? Then my problems would have been over.'

'Maybe he would have done if he'd lived a bit longer!'

They both turned, astonished, at the sound of Frankie's voice as she marched into the room.

'Who the hell——?' Cal's eyes narrowed. 'Oh, it's you.' His gaze ran down over her loosely brushed

topknot, her skimpy top and exuberant skirt. She knew
she looked young and tanned and healthy, and met his
eyes levelly as he scrutinised her, but she still felt a jolt
as their gazes snagged.

'"My, what a change is here",' he quoted slowly,
and a faint teasing warmth crept into his grey look.

'What do you mean?'

'I mean you look quite different from yesterday.
Yesterday you looked like a librarian.' His mouth
crooked at her.

'Can I help you?' Elaine Pye cut in quickly, and her
look was certainly not warmer. Her mouth set in clear
disapproval as she looked at Frankie's bare midriff and
long, slender legs.

'I left a bag here yesterday. Over by the window. It's
a present for my aunt. I came to pick it up.'

'I wouldn't have recognised you,' Cal said.

'Yesterday was my aunt's idea—my interview outfit.'

'And this is the real you?'

She shrugged. 'I wear what I feel comfortable in.'

Suddenly he levered himself away from the mantelpiece and came over to her. He took her chin in his
thumb and forefinger and pushed her head this way,
then that, examining her. She smelt a musky clean
smell from his skin and saw the dark shadow of his
beard. His eyes scrutinised her face with a gaze as
impersonal as a camera lens. 'You look exactly like
your father, you know. It shows with your hair off your
face like that. Same eyes. Same chin. Probably the
same dreadful sense of humour.'

She found she needed to swallow as he dropped his
hand, and her own hand went up to rub at the place
where his fingers had held her tightly. 'I don't know

about that. I can't seem to find much to laugh about at the moment.'

'Oh?' He raised a casual eyebrow. 'You've got youth, health, beauty—maybe even brains for all I know. That would be enough for most people.'

'You can't live off youth and health. They don't pay the bills.'

'And you can't get a job? I find that hard to believe.'

'Oh, I can get one all right! I can get hundreds. The trouble is they're all the same. Typing and filing and dictation. And who wants to work in an office all day——?'

Beside her she heard Elaine Pye snort disapprovingly, and she turned to her. 'I'm sorry if that sounds rude, but it's just how I feel.' She swung back to Cal. 'I get in in the morning, and by coffee-time I feel as if the walls are closing in on me. I feel so restless all the time I could scream, but no one seems to understand! I often think there must be something wrong with me. I can't seem to accept what everyone else seems perfectly happy with: the daily routine, the same thing over and over again. I want so much more but I don't know how to get it!'

His eyes held hers. He seemed mildly amused by her outburst. 'It isn't a crime to want more.' He turned to his secretary. 'Elaine, I think I can hear the phone——'

Elaine crossed the room, found the Harrods carrier-bag and dumped it down at her feet like an invitation to leave. 'I believe this is what you came for. Would you mind letting yourself out?'

Frankie turned to watch her depart. 'I've offended her, haven't I?'

'Probably. She is a secretary, after all.'

'I didn't mean to.'

'It doesn't matter. She's very easily offended—and very easily gets over it again.'

'I tend to speak my mind.'

'It's an O'Shea habit that I remember very well. Your father once told me I had the arrogance of an elephant and the ability of a mouse.'

She laughed.

He turned and began to pick up some sheets of contact prints. 'He was right, too; it's been one of the greatest regrets of my life that he hasn't been here to tell.' He looked at her and suddenly his voice was deadly serious. 'I owed your father a lot. More than anyone in the world knows. I always wished I could have repaid that debt.'

She hesitated, then burst out impulsively, 'You could—by giving me the job.'

He looked up sharply.

'I heard you talking just now. I know you haven't found anyone. I'm strong and willing. I'd work hard. And I'd love to see Africa. I've been thinking about it all night.'

'But I explained the circumstances to you——'

She shrugged scornfully. 'Things have changed. Women do everything men do and more. I could do the job as well as any man.'

'And you think your father would thank me for hauling you off alone into bush——'

'My father was very unconventional. He never bothered about appearances, only the truth of things. If you're worrying what people might think. . .'

'It's not something that's ever handicapped me so far,' he said drily. 'But even so——'

'Even so, what? I know I could do the job as well as anyone.'

He straightened up and looked at her, his eyes calculating. There was a long pause. She held her breath, wondering what he was thinking behind that dark, direct stare. Then he rapped out, 'Could you drive on rough tracks?'

'I've been driving a Land Rover on the local farm since I was fifteen. I helped with the lambing every Easter.'

'And suppose I had to leave you alone for a night or so? Camping in the bush?'

She lifted her chin. 'I haven't got any experience. But I'd manage. I learn fast.'

There was another long pause. She scarcely breathed while his eyes scoured her.

'You know,' he said slowly, 'I'm beginning to think you would.'

'Then give me a chance.'

He raked a hand through his hair. 'It's not what I intended. Taking a little convent girl with me.'

'I'm not a little convent girl! I never fitted in there either! That was another of Aunt Jenny's ideas.'

His grey eyes scoured her.

'You said you wanted to repay my father,' she urged. 'My father wanted me to be happy. And I'm not! Not at all. My aunt—she's my guardian—is a lovely person, but she just doesn't understand the sort of person I am. She wants me to be a nice, sweet, normal sort of girl and I'm not any of those things! She wants me to wear twin-sets and do a little job in the local town until I get married and settle down, but I don't want to settle down!'

'What do you want, then?'

She lifted her chin and said stubbornly, 'Right now I want to come to Africa with you.'

He stared back at her until she almost quailed. 'Tell me,' he said slowly, 'why do I feel I'm being bullied?'

Because you are, she thought silently, but she only looked at him, not speaking. He held her wide-eyed, stubborn gaze for what seemed like eternity. She forced herself not to look away.

'All right, then,' he snapped eventually. 'You're on. But don't blame me if it doesn't work out.'

CHAPTER THREE

FRANKIE could feel Cal's dark eyes on her as she struggled towards him across the airport concourse.

'What in hell is that?' he said scathingly as she dumped her burden at his feet, panting.

'It's a suitcase.'

A flight announcement boomed out, drowning her words. She swallowed, defensive under his cutting gaze. 'I *know* it's not exactly the thing for bashing about the bush, but I didn't have anything else, and it's been such a rush to get organised in time.'

'They certainly won't let you take it on board as hand baggage.'

She looked at him. He wore jeans and a light jacket, and carried only a camera bag and a small battered holdall. He was obviously an experienced traveller, entirely cool and at ease in the milling chaos of the busy terminal, whereas she felt hot and flustered and decidedly apprehensive.

'Is that a problem?'

'It means we'll have to hang around at the other end while they unload the plane.' His look told her what he thought about that.

'Well, I'm sorry!' she said, tetchy with nerves, 'but if I'd had a bit more information—like where exactly we're going, and how long for—I might have been able to travel a bit lighter. As it is, I've had to pack for every contingency I could think of, and a few more besides.'

He scowled at her tone. 'Well, I'm sorry about that, but, as you so rightly point out, there's been no time for anything. For one thing I've been dashing all over the place. I've hardly been in London since I last saw you. Anyway, here are your travel documents. And here's a brief itinerary that Elaine typed up for you. It should tell you all you need to know.'

Frankie took the papers wordlessly.

'I've already checked in,' he said abruptly, 'so if you'll excuse me, there's some phone calls I have to make. I expect I'll see you on the plane.'

With a sinking heart she watched his disappearing back, realising that he had no intention of helping her with the unfamiliar check-in procedures. In fact, he could not seem to get away from her fast enough, and it was at least an hour later before she saw him again. As they waited to board the plane he came over to where she sat reading through the document he had given her.

'OK?'

'Oh, fine.' She veiled the sarcasm in her voice. The itinerary could not have been sparser or more impersonal. '04.08 a.m. arrive Nairobi,' it started, 'transfer to overnight accommodation', and continued in much the same vein for its ten brief paragraphs. It could have been the agenda for a meeting of sales reps, she thought, or the outline of a marketing conference.

'What's "associated gamepark activity"?'

'What?' He frowned.

'It says here, "Drive to Masai Mara to photograph

game and associated gamepark activity for International Wildlife Fund".'

His eyes flicked shrewdly over hers. 'She shouldn't have bothered to put that in. It just means any old thing that comes up. I've got an open brief.' His voice was casual, but she saw that his eyes had darkened with wariness.

She folded the paper away. 'You mean the driver gets kept in the dark,' she said bluntly.

Their eyes met in open antagonism. He bent towards her. 'The driver,' he said, very coldly and very deliberately, 'is here to drive. Nothing more. Nothing less.' He held her eyes with a hard look, but she refused to be intimidated and kept her own open green gaze on his. 'Look, Frankie,' he burst out harshly, scything the air with his hand, 'let's get one thing clear right from the start. I normally travel alone and I like it that way. I don't like having to have your help, I don't welcome your company, and I have no intention whatsoever of turning this trip into a social jaunt. Do you understand?'

Her eyes sparked with anger and colour flushed to her cheeks, but she swallowed back her fury as best she could. 'I'm not here to socialise,' she said tersely. 'A little politeness would be quite enough.'

'Even that's probably asking too much,' he said coldly. 'Social niceties have never been my strong point, and, anyway, when I'm working it's work that I think about. Nothing else.' And he got up and pointedly sat down in a seat some way away from her.

She watched him, furious, and suddenly wished with all her heart that she had never set eyes on him. Then she deliberately raised her book high in front of her face and did not look in his direction again until the flight was called.

On the plane they were apart, too. Cal pushed past where she was sitting and claimed a seat across the aisle, two rows in front, although he was neither out of sight nor mind since his profile was easily visible.

Which was a pity, she thought grimly, because she very much wanted to enjoy this trip as much as she could, despite the strained circumstances. Yet every time she glanced up she was forced to see his dark figure, and seethed with righteous anger at the brutal rudeness of his behaviour towards her.

Over the top of her plastic meal-tray she watched him wave away all food and drink and settle down in his seat to sleep. He seemed to drop off instantly, even before the cabin lights were dimmed, yet later, in the deep hours of the night, as the plane droned over the darkened desert below, she woke up and saw him also awake, a brooding figure staring into space, lost in the thread of his own thoughts.

In the dusky light she saw eyes as dark as stone, a stubborn hawk-like face and a hard, sensual mouth, and wondered what restless, turning thoughts had woken him.

She still knew so little about him, despite diligent efforts on her part to unearth whatever information she could find. Back in Yorkshire, where she had made a flying visit after he had given her the job, she had immediately enlisted the help of an old school-friend who worked in the library at the local television company, and had spent an afternoon reading through a stack of yellowing newspaper cuttings. The friend had also arranged for her to see a video of a documentary programme about him that had been made two years ago.

She had sat alone in the darkened viewing-booth watching Cal dodging mortar attacks in the Far East, Cal photographing flooded villages in Asia, Cal, grimy and exhausted, sprawled asleep in a lorry full of soldiers. He looked as tough and handsome as any Hollywood version of a war photographer, but he also looked utterly private and self-contained, she thought. The director of the film had been unable to win an interview with him, and had had to rely on the impressions of friends and colleagues, so that the only hard information she had gained from her entire afternoon's researches was that Cal Fenton was thirty-two, single, a known womaniser, and completely devoted to his work, which had won him several fistfuls of awards and international prizes.

Although, she thought, as she watched him shift his long legs restlessly in the cramped airline seat, there had been one brief moment when the film had seemed to capture a different side of him.

He had been visiting an orphanage in India, and as the sad little scraps of children had crowded round him he had squatted in the dust among them and let them jostle close to him and finger his camera with wonder. And as he reached out his hand to a small boy hanging back in the crowd she had seen, for one fleeting second, deep tenderness and compassion in his eyes.

But perhaps it had been an illusion, she thought. Perhaps she had seen those emotions simply because she had wanted to. Certainly nothing in his curt manner today indicated any sign of a warmer human being hidden deep within his obnoxious shell.

Her thoughts moved restlessly until she became aware that the engine noise was changing, and the plane slowly began its long descent towards their destination.

The airport was deserted, but, even so, the luggage took forever to arrive on the carousel, and as luck would have it her suitcase was the very last item to come out. Cal had already marched on ahead and was clearly seething with impatience by the time she straggled out through Customs to join him.

'In here.' He pushed her into a taxi. 'For goodness' sake let's get going.'

The car roared off down the road. He sat in silence beside her. Clutching her courage in both hands, she said, 'Cal?'

'What is it?'

'If you were me, what would you pack for this trip?'

He looked at her, surprised. 'Shorts and T-shirts. Maybe a pair of trousers, a sweater. Sunglasses. Insect repellent. A book.'

'That's all?'

He shrugged. 'Washing powder. The usual basics. Some people find a corkscrew essential.'

She smiled. 'Like Mike. He never went anywhere without his Swiss army knife.'

'I remember.' His face set hard, as if the last thing on earth he wanted to talk about was her father. 'Why are you asking?'

'I'm just trying to work out what to jettison.'

'It's a bit late now. There'll be room enough in the Land Rover for your case.'

'It's not that. It's how I feel—all encumbered and amateurish.'

'Well, you are, aren't you?' His eyes glittered as he glanced across the dark car towards her. 'I'll lay odds you've never been further than the Costa Brava before.'

'Not even that,' she admitted ruefully. 'Aunt Jenny always had a soft spot for Bridlington.' Her eyes skimmed the blackness outside the windows of the taxi 'I can't believe it's actually Africa out there.'

'Suburban Nairobi isn't exactly the furthest-flung corner of the earth.'

'It might not be to you, but to me it's as exotic as the upper reaches of the White Nile.'

She heard him sigh slightly. 'I hope I haven't been rash, bringing you along, Frankie.'

'Because of my naïveté? I can easily pretend a world-weary cynicism, if you'd rather. It just wouldn't be true!' She flung herself back in her seat, muttering to herself, 'Anyway, you've got enough for both of us.'

'What?'

'Nothing.'

He flashed her an angry glance. 'Naïveté I can live with. Childishness, I'm not so sure.'

They rode in a charged silence to the hotel, a low colonial-style building set in spreading gardens, and Cal paid the driver, banged the taxi door and marched on ahead. He plunged his hand down on to the bell, summoning a bleary-eyed desk clerk.

'Mr and Mrs Fenton,' he rapped out, 'and look sharp about it. We'd like to catch at least a few hours' sleep in what's left of tonight.'

'What?'

She could scarcely believe what she had just heard. Cal quelled her with a look that chilled her to her marrow.

'Room 205. If you'll sign here I'll show you the way.' The clerk scratched his stomach and regarded them without curiosity. Cal signed impatiently in a brisk, bold hand. Then the clerk picked up their bags and led them off down an open cloistered corridor. Exotic blossoms scented the warm night air, but she scarcely noticed them in her agitation, which burst out the minute the door closed behind them.

'What the hell do you think you're doing?'

Cal turned and faced her. 'I'm going to bed. I'm shattered.'

'Mr and Mrs Fenton!'

'For heaven's sake, Frankie, stop acting like a teenager. Society here isn't as sophisticated as it could be. I wasn't prepared to get into any aggravation about us having different names when we're sharing a room. Not at this time of night, anyway.'

'What?' She felt stupid with tiredness and dislocation. In the bright light of the room, Cal looked drawn, and she guessed she did, too. 'Sharing a room——'

'Oh, for God's sake!' He raked a hand through his hair. 'I told you. I told you all this in London, the very first time we met. I couldn't have spelled it out more clearly. That's why I needed a man for this job. But you still insisted a girl could do it, and I was desperate enough to take you at your word. I'm beginning to think it was a grave mistake——'

'Did you? Tell me, I mean.' Her green eyes searched his face doubtfully.

'I did,' he bit out. 'I told you the International

Wildlife Society were paying for the trip, and that I had to keep costs to an absolute minimum.'

Her face showed her doubts. All she could remember was him telling her he was going to Africa, and the idea infusing her with such a sudden rush of enthusiasm that she had scarcely heard another word he had said. Even so. . .

'And in case you're wondering why I don't fork out and pay for another room myself,' he went on, as if reading her mind, 'it's because I don't see the need. You told me you could do the same job as a man, and I'm taking your word for it. You can have my absolute guarantee that I won't be taking any advantage of the situation——' His eyes ripped over hers and his mouth crooked with cold humour '—and I trust I can expect the same from you.'

'Oh, yes. I promise I won't ravage you in the middle of the night,' she said miserably. The room was clean, but small, and the twin beds were separated by nothing but a tiny bedside-table.

He followed her look and sighed harshly. 'Frankie, you'd better get used to it. We're going to be spending an awful lot of time together.' His eyes registered her lonely bleakness, but his look did not soften one bit.

She put her suitcase down slowly on the bed and took a deep breath. 'I'm used to it,' she said dully, and his eyes sparked at her tone.

'Good.' He shrugged his jacket back on. 'Now I'm going out for a five-minute walk. That should give you time to get to bed.'

'You don't have to——'

'I know I don't. I'm choosing to. If there's one thing

I don't feel up to tonight it's squirming schoolgirl modesty. Goodnight.'

'Goodnight.' And good riddance, she mouthed silently, as the door banged behind him.

She washed and changed with indecent haste and was lying in darkness with the covers up to her nose when he came back in. He went to the bathroom. She pulled the covers over her head, tense as a bow-string. Soon he came out. She heard him walk past her bed, heard the rustle of cloth, the rasp of a zip as he undressed. The noises were shockingly close, indecently intimate. She wanted to gasp or giggle to release her tension. Then, tired and strained, she felt an overwhelming longing to be back safely tucked up in her own room at home again.

Why had she ever thought Yorkshire was dull? Or Aunt Jenny stifling? What was she doing here, alone in Africa, in uncomfortable proximity to the chilly likes of Cal Fenton?

She heard his bedsprings creak, heard him shift once or twice, then very quickly heard the deep, regular breathing of sleep. Slowly she untensed her muscles, and relaxed her posture. Cal must have learnt to sleep anywhere, under almost any circumstances, she thought, on planes and trains, in battles and bush camps. And no doubt there was nothing remotely strange to him about sharing his room with a woman.

Whereas to her. . . She opened her eyes, but the room was in pitch darkness. She could only sense, not see, the alien humped figure in the bed near by. To her, sharing a room with any man was an entirely new experience, let alone a man as mean and moody and dangerous as Cal Fenton.

CHAPTER FOUR

THE birds woke Frankie up, singing an exotic chorus outside the window. She opened her eyes and remembered exactly where she was, and why. The light outside the window was bright, and she could hear maids clattering their buckets and brooms in the corridor outside. She looked at her watch. Eight o'clock. Quietly, she turned on her side and looked across to Cal's bed.

He lay deeply asleep. Some time in the night he had pushed the sheet down so that it now only half covered his hips. One arm was bent above his head, the other lay at his side.

She elbowed herself up and stared at him; she could not stop herself, there was such grace and strength in the lines of his body. His back was broad and brown, its close-packed muscles dipping to the narrowness of his hips, and his skin looked so warm and smooth that she wanted to reach out and touch it, just as the morning sun touched his hair and put the sheen of a starling's wing in its thick darkness. She swallowed. He was flawless, a perfect specimen of the male of the species. Or he would have been except for two small but deep scars that marked the muscle of one shoulder-blade.

She looked at them, then at his sleeping face. Were they the bullet wounds that had shattered his bones? Were those small marks the very reason that she was lying here, in this strange bed, in this strange continent?

'Yes, that's right.'

She jumped a mile at his deep, lazy voice.

'What——?'

'You were wondering if those scars were the cause of all this trouble. You've been studying me as if I was a carcass on a slab.'

He still seemed asleep, but when she looked more closely she could see that his eyes were open the merest fraction.

'I thought you were asleep!'

'I know.' He rolled over, stretching his arms and yawning. She saw a powerful chest, sprinkled with dark hair, and looked away. 'It's a useful skill, being able to play dead while having a good look round at the same time. It's come in handy on more than one occasion.'

'I'm surprised you aren't *covered* in scars, leading the life you do.'

'A tan can cover a multitude of sins.'

He turned his head sideways on the pillow, his eyes glinting, and observed casually, 'You know, if you always look like that in the morning, you're going to give me a lot of trouble sticking to the letter of our agreement.'

'What do you mean?'

He rolled his eyes, not speaking, and she looked down, then blushed furiously as she realised that her supposedly decorous pyjamas were unbuttoned almost to the waist, and that as she had leant up on her elbow to look at him she had been virtually naked to his gaze.

She lay flat, raking the sheets up to her neck. He

looked at his watch and groaned. 'Three hours' sleep is definitely not enough. Did you sleep?'

'Like a log.'

'Not too disturbed by your new marital status after all?'

She laughed, then admitted, 'Well, a bit. I didn't drop off as quickly as you.'

'I'll wager it's the first time in your life you've slept with a man,' he observed casually.

'I wouldn't waste your money,' she bit back sharply. 'My private life stays just that—private.'

'You mean you don't mix work and pleasure? Well, that's a philosophy I entirely approve of. Now.' He moved a hand to his sheet and looked across at her. 'I plan to get up, and since I haven't a stitch on I suggest you preserve your maidenly modesty by shutting your eyes.'

She did meekly as she was told, and when he returned from the bathroom he was decently clad in bush-shirt and jeans, looking fresh and alert and ready to face the day.

'I'm going to be busy all day,' he said, checking his wallet and papers.

'What shall I do?'

'Two things. First pick up our Land Rover. I'll leave the address here. Then get us some stores; we'll need enough for a week in the bush. I'll leave the money here as well.' He put money and papers on the table. 'I'd also get some more sleep, if I were you. You may need some in the bank over the next few days.' His eyes went over her, swiftly taking in her auburn curls spread on the pillow, then he strode to the door. 'OK?'

'Yes. But——' she sat up in bed '—when you say

stores——' It was useless. The door had closed on him before she had even framed the first of her myriad questions.

Well, she was on her own, but to her surprise the prospect did not daunt her in the least. Too excited to sleep further, she dressed in trousers and a T-shirt and went to have breakfast on the veranda. The sun warmed her skin and the strange scents of the city delighted her as she sat chewing on her pen and drawing up a shopping-list.

'Do you have a map of the city?' she asked the desk-clerk.

'Oh, yes, Mrs Fenton,' he said, producing one, and she stifled a giggle at the unfamiliar name.

The garage was a short walk away. She went into the office. 'You've got a Land Rover for Mr Fenton. I'm picking it up.'

There were a mass of forms to fill in. 'Your name, please?' said the owner.

She hesitated. 'Mrs Fenton. Mrs Frankie Fenton.'

'Your driving licence, please.' She handed it over. He frowned. 'This says O'Shea.'

'My maiden name. I've only just got married. You can check on me at the hotel if you want.'

'OK,' the man said slowly, then smiled. 'A honeymoon in the bush, eh? What could be more romantic?'

A lot, she thought to herself, an awful lot. But she smiled diplomatically and picked up the keys.

At the garage she enquired about shops, and from there pioneered her way to the city's main supermarket. It was small and sparsely stocked compared to its English equivalents, but by dint of diligent searching she was able to put together enough basics to see them through. The few vegetables that were bagged for sale were limp and expensive, but across the street was a market, where turbanned ladies sat on colourful cloths with their goods spread out before them. She locked the boxes of supplies into the back of the Land Rover and set off across the street, drawn by the bustle and colour. For a time she simply walked around, looking and listening, then she launched herself into the drama of bartering, armed to the teeth with her father's Irish blarney and her laughing, good-humoured eyes.

The market mamas responded loudly and cheerfully to this slip of a girl with the flashing smiles and the spirit to drive a good bargain, and they delegated an army of small children to carry her purchases back to her jeep. She gave them some coins, then headed back to the market and bought herself a long-handled woven basket, big enough to hold the few clothes she would need for a week. Let him complain about this, she thought grimly as she settled it on her shoulder and went back to the car.

Driving back to the hotel, a sign caught her eyes. 'The African Camping and Supplies Co'. She frowned. Was she responsible for hiring a tent, sleeping-bags, a stove? Was that included in 'stores'? Cal had been infuriatingly uninformative.

Yet when she got back she found that a large mound of bundles from the self-same shop had already been delivered to their room. She explored them, thinking hard, trying to project with her imagination what it would be like in the bush. Then she drove back to town and bought a powerful torch and spare batteries, and a first-aid kit.

It was late before she finally returned to the hotel

that day. There was no one in the room, so she washed quickly and went down to the veranda. Cal was there, already halfway through dinner, but to her surprise he was not alone. She walked across to him and felt his dark eyes taking in her figure.

'Ah, Frankie!' He turned to his companions. 'There you are, gentlemen,' he said expansively. 'You ask me what I'm doing in Africa——' He left the sentence hanging. She looked at him in astonishment. He seemed to have been drinking, and his companions certainly had. They leered at her with glistening eyes.

'Geoff Peters from the American Press Service. Murray Boulter of Reuters,' he introduced them. 'They're having a little trouble believing I'm only here to take animal pictures. I told them it was pleasure as well as business, but they didn't seem to believe me.'

The fatter of the two men snorted. 'The day you go on a pleasure trip, Fenton, is the day I turn in my press-pass. There's something fishy behind all this——'

'If that's what you want to waste your time thinking,' Cal said smoothly and caught her hand in his, drawing her towards him. 'It's late. I was worried,' he said in an undertone, and his voice was sharp and serious.

She felt bewildered by the touch of his hand holding hers, by his new affability and seemingly genuine anxiety.

'I went out for a drive this afternoon in the Land Rover. It's a good job I did. There was a slow puncture on the front nearside wheel.'

'What did you do?'

'I changed it. I had to, to get back to town. Then I went back to the garage and made them give me another spare. They didn't want to. They had to get one from another garage, but I told them we were leaving at dawn. I just sort of sat there until they had to do it.'

His eyes stripped over hers in astonishment. Tonight they didn't seem a bit bleak, she thought, just grey and impossibly handsome. She swallowed and pulled her hand away, frightened that he would feel how her pulses were suddenly racing beneath his look and his touch. Cal's glance lingered on her for a moment, then he knocked back his drink. 'You see, boys,' he said, winking at his companions, 'a stunning redhead who can change the tyre of a Land Rover. I think I've finally found the answer to my dreams.'

'But are you the answer to hers?' the tall man drawled. He looked at Frankie. 'He does tend to stand in the way of flying bullets, this man of yours.'

She suddenly felt sick, standing like an exhibit, in the middle of a lie, with Cal talking about her as if she were his property, and she turned to the man with venom. 'You don't need to tell me anything about flying bullets, I know exactly what they can do! Especially to people who make a habit of hanging out in dangerous places. People like my father!' She shot a bitter glance at Cal, exhausted from her long day and furious at the confusion he was causing her. 'My father was a foreign correspondent, like you,' she bit out, her gaze stripping round the table. 'He covered the war in the Middle East. For years he was lucky. He dodged bullets and side-stepped mines. But in the end he walked into a car bomb, and that was the end of him.' Her glittering gaze came to rest on Cal, who was watching her closely, but as her eyes locked with his he looked quickly away and reached for his drink.

'Calm down, sit down, and eat something,' he commanded.

'No, thank you. It would stick in my throat!' she said, and, turning on her heel, she began to walk away.

As she did, she heard voices erupt in an excited chorus behind her.

'Good God!' she heard one say, 'That's O'Shea's girl you've got there! You've got the cheek of the devil——'

And another said, 'Of course, you were there, weren't you, Fenton, when it happened?'

Then there was Cal's voice, sharp and forbidding, cutting through the babble, and then she walked on, too tired and drained to care about anything except reaching the room and falling into the blessed oblivion of sleep.

It was later, much later, when she woke up to the sound of slurred voices outside the bedroom.

'You lucky blighter,' one of them was chuckling. 'Has she got any sisters—?'

And another interrupted, 'Fat lot of use you'd be to any woman tonight, Peters, after your skinful.'

Then she heard Cal's voice saying, 'If she had, I'd make sure I kept them away from the likes of you.'

There was more talk, more bursts of laughter, then she heard a hand on the doorknob as a voice said, 'Sweet dreams, Fenton—if you get any sleep at all, that is.' She heard Cal laugh, low and huskily under his breath, amid a burst of raucous guffaws; then he came in. He shut the door behind him and leaned against it, listening.

'You're not asleep, Frankie. Stop pretending.'

'I was. I still would be if it wasn't for that racket outside!' She kept her eyes tight shut.

She heard him come over and sit on his bed, facing her.

'You're mad at me.'

'Of course I'm mad at you! Talking about me as if I'm some—I don't know—bit of stuff you've brought along for a ride.'

He leaned over to snap on her bedside-light. She opened her eyes and sat up, swiftly checking her pyjama buttons for decency.

'That's a somewhat unfortunate turn of phrase, under the circumstances.' She saw his eyes glint in the low light, his lips crook, and to her consternation she felt a wriggle of response to him under her skin. He was such a handsome man, and clearly experienced in using his charms for whatever ends suited his purpose.

'You're drunk!'

'Nonsense, I'm as sober as a judge. It's just useful to pretend to be, with old soaks like those two.'

'Just like it's useful to pretend I'm your latest girl-friend?' she said scornfully.

'Do you honestly believe simple-minded souls like those two would believe anything different? Man plus woman only adds up to one thing in their book, especially when the two concerned are sharing a room. Anyway,' he added brusquely, 'I wanted them off my back.'

'And just what does that mean?'

'What I say. I don't want them sniffing around my every movement, hoping they get on to a good story.'

She scoured his eyes. 'Is that because you are? On to a good story?'

'If I was, I wouldn't be saying.'

'Not even to your girlfriend?' she taunted. 'Your wife? Or is she only good for one thing?'

He sighed and his expression hardened. He stood up, and began to unbutton his shirt. 'Forget it, Frankie. It's late, and I'm tired. I don't see that there's any crime in saying you're a stunning redhead, since it's patently true—and I always believe in making use of the resources to hand.'

A flush of warmth went through her. A stunning redhead. Her eyes were riveted to the progress of his fingers down the line of his buttons. Dark hair curled at the opening of his shirt. She blinked and pushed back her hair. 'And what would you have done if it had been a boy you were travelling with? Said the same sort of things?'

His teeth gleamed as he grinned. 'I don't think they would have believed me. They're old hands. We've been around together a long time.'

'You mean they've seen your women come and go?'

He shrugged. 'They know enough to know I'm a normal red-blooded male.'

'Oh!' She flung herself back on the pillows. 'I really hate all this!'

'I don't know why you're getting so worked up.'

'Don't you?' She shot up again, eyes sparking. 'Then I'll tell you.' She put up her hands and began to tick off her fingers. 'In my first job, dear old Mr Holden, Aunt Jenny's trusted solicitor, spent his days peering down my dress and patting my knees. In my second job, my boss harassed me so much that I finally had to leave——'

'Well, what do you expect with looks like yours? Have you ever studied yourself in a mirror? That's what life's going to be like for you, so you'd better learn how to handle it with a bit of grace.'

'What I expect is to be allowed to get on with my life in peace! It isn't much to ask. I thought this job, at least, would be different!'

He froze in the act of pulling off his shirt and his eyes ripped over her. 'Have I made a pass at you?'

'No,' she conceded grudgingly.

'Well, then, stop complaining.'

'But you still treat me as if I'm your property. All those things you were saying tonight——'

'Oh, for God's sake!' He finished ripping off his shirt and threw it impatiently over a chair. He stood bare-torsoed with his hands on his hips, staring down at her. 'I said those things just to keep those two old hacks quiet, since they clearly weren't willing to believe I was just here to take pretty animal pictures. If I'd had a young lad with me I'd have devised some other story. I'd have said he was my godson and I'd always promised to take him camping in the bush, or something. It isn't worth all this fuss!' He bent down and began to unlace his shoes. Then his eye caught the camping gear and boxes of stores, and he abruptly changed tack.

'You got everything?'

'I think so,' she said, still sullen. He eyed her darkly, but all he said was, 'Did you really change that tyre?'

'Yes.'

'Without help?'

'Yes. Of course.' It had been a terrible struggle, and

there had been times when she had feared she didn't have the strength to turn the wheel-brace, but she wasn't going to tell him that.

'Then I take my hat off to you.' He took off his shoes and socks and headed barefoot towards the bathroom. But by her bed he paused and looked intently down at her.

'Frankie, I'll tell you straight. If you're going to give me this sort of trouble all the time, I'd rather send you back to London right now.'

'And who'd do your driving?'

'I'd find someone.'

She swallowed, then summoned enough spirit to meet his glare with a direct look. 'I won't cause you any trouble if you'll simply stop treating me as an object. So far I've either been an unwelcome bit of baggage you've had to cart along for the trip, a pretend wife, or a stunning redhead who's the answer to all your dreams. I don't like any of those roles, I'd rather be myself. And if I can't be that, then I'll go home tomorrow, and gladly!'

He looked at her for a long, long time, until she felt her heart lurch up hard into her chest at the dark steel of his look.

'You certainly drive a tough bargain.'

'That's what they said in the market today.'

'I thought *I* was the employer.'

'You are. But these days employees have rights, too; haven't you heard?'

'I'm hearing it now. Loud and clear.' He was still looking darkly at her. She wanted to swallow, but she didn't.

'Well.' she challenged him.

He sighed. 'What can I say? I'll do my best,' he said, 'but I can't promise more than that. Because the truth is, Frankie, I don't want you here. I don't want anyone here. As I've already told you, when I'm working, I like to work alone. And anyone else is just a millstone round my neck.'

CHAPTER FIVE

'FRANKIE.' Something was shaking her.

'Mmm?' She swam up through sleep. Cal was gripping her shoulder impatiently.

'Wake up.'

'What?'

It was still dark in the room, but he was already washed and dressed. She could smell a faint tang of shaving foam and toothpaste.

'Time to get up. I want an early start. I'm going to open up the Land Rover.'

She blinked her way awake. Her watch said five. Fumbling, she went to the bathroom and washed. It was astonishing, she thought, how deeply and peacefully she had slept, how miraculously rested and refreshed she felt, considering that unpleasant scene last night. Perhaps she'd been unfair on him, she thought with fresh benevolence as she scrubbed her teeth, and she nodded sagely to herself in the mirror. After all, it was obviously just as much a strain for him to travel in tandem like this as it was for her.

She went back out, pulling off her pyjamas, and began to dress. She put on a pair of pants and looked round for her T-shirt. At that very moment the door opened, and Cal marched in. She turned, surprised, a slight figure in the skimpiest white briefs. He took in her naked form, her high breasts and slim hips, at a glance. Then he snapped his eyes away, picked up a box of supplies, and walked out.

It was over in seconds, leaving her shaken and angry. How dared he just barge back in like that? she thought. He should have knocked! He should have realised she would have been dressing! Yet as she quickly pulled on her shorts and T-shirt she knew there was another strand to her anger. It was the blankness, the utter uninterest she had seen in his face as he had looked her over. Last night he had called her a stunning redhead, yet this morning he had surveyed her as coolly as if she were a lump of wood. He'd seen her virtually naked and it had not caused him as much as the blink of an eye.

But that was because she wasn't a woman to him, she realised. She was just a slip of a girl. And maybe not even that. She was an assistant, someone simply to be instructed, or used, or ignored, as circumstances dictated. Oh! He was the most infuriating man!

Angrily she crammed her few clothes into the basket and rolled a towel over the top to keep everything in place. Nothing seemed to penetrate his mask, his tough self-sufficiency, yet the more she saw of him the more she felt the urge to try to break through his reserve to find the man beneath.

There was a polite knock at the door.

'It's a bit late for that!' she snapped.

A puzzled waiter came in with a tray of coffee and rolls. 'Mr Fenton, he ordered this breakfast,' said the man, eyeing her warily.

'Oh. Thank you. Put it in there, would you?'

Cal walked in as the man walked out.

'You could have knocked——' she burst out, but he put up a silencing hand.

'Leave it,' he snapped. 'I don't want another scene.'

Her mouth shut mutinously. He poured coffee—just one cup, she noticed, for himself—and drank it in one draught before picking up the tent. In the doorway he paused, as if her angry vibrations were rays that pierced his back. Then he turned and looked at her, his grey eyes cold.

'Look,' he said angrily. 'Where we're going there are no doors, no walls, no bathrooms—nothing. So you might as well shed that convent modesty of yours right now.'

'It's nothing to do with the convent. It's just normal!'

'These aren't normal circumstances.' He sighed impatiently. 'Look, Frankie, understand this. I've lived alongside all sorts of people, in circumstances you couldn't even begin to imagine. The sight of a normal, naked girl isn't going to shock me, or inflame me to uncontrolled lust!' He grinned grimly. 'Especially not at this unearthly hour of the morning.'

'Good! That's fine for you, then, isn't it? But what about me? What about how *I* feel? Last night you said you'd try and treat me as a person. But this morning you didn't even bother to show me the most basic courtesy!'

His eyes flickered over her with clear dislike.

'All right, I apologise. I could have knocked, I agree. I just happened to be thinking about something completely different at the time. I'm not used to travelling with someone else, as I've already explained, and I'm sure my manners leave a lot to be desired.' His mouth set angrily. 'God dammit, I knew a woman would be nothing but trouble!'

Frankie lowered her eyes. He had a point. He hadn't wanted to bring her. It was she who had persuaded him, protesting that she could easily do as good a job as a man. And now she was throwing exactly the sort of female tantrum he had obviously foreseen and dreaded.

'Well, maybe we've both got a lot to learn,' she said, with grudging grace. 'I'll help you load the Land Rover.'

They left the city just as it was stirring to life, and were soon driving through the kind of landscapes that she had dreamed of. The bush stretched away in all directions, green and brown and studded with flat-topped acacias. Hornbills with long tails perched on rocks at the side of the road, and distant hills broke the horizon and beckoned them on.

She drove carefully and was aware of Cal slowly relaxing into his seat next to her, although whether it was because of her steady driving, or because they were finally shaking the dust of the city from their feet, she could not tell.

'Damn,' he muttered once.

'What is it?' She glanced across at him, his regular profile and long limbs sprawled gracefully in the seat.

'I forgot to get another torch. We ought to have a spare, for emergencies.'

'I bought one. And spare batteries.'

'You did?' He turned with surprise, then smiled, and again her heart dipped strangely because he was unbearably handsome when his face relaxed into warmth. 'Well done.' She basked like a cat in his approval.

'I tried to think of everything, but it's not easy when you've never done this before.'

'If your quartermastering is as good as your driving it'll be fine.'

Again her heart warmed. Two compliments in two minutes! She suddenly wanted to sing.

'But I bet there's something you did forget.' His eyes glinted at her.

'What's that?'

'The beers.'

'Oh. No. I mean yes. I forgot them.'

'Don't worry. We'll get some somewhere. There's nothing like a cold beer to drive the dust from your throat at the end of the day.'

Later, on the long, hot drive Cal made her stop by a ramshackle roadside store, jumped down and came out with a heavy box of cans and bottles. She helped him fill the cool-box, and he lifted the rest into the back of the Land Rover.

'Should you be doing that, with your bad shoulder?'

He grimaced and rubbed it. 'Probably not. It's a damn nuisance.'

'Will it be all right again, in time?'

He opened two cans, and they leaned against the side of the vehicle, swigging companionably. 'I may have to have it reset. The Haitian doctor wasn't exactly out of Harley Street.' He looked round at the huge horizon and the white clouds that floated like giant saucers in the sky, and deftly deflected the conversation away from his injuries. 'I love Africa. It does wonders for the soul.'

'Soul?' she echoed doubtfully. Could such a thing exist in a hardened creature like Cal Fenton? 'Are you really only going to be taking wildlife pictures, Cal?'

He gave her a long, sideways look. 'I'm going to be taking wildlife pictures.'

'That's not what I asked.'

'I know. But that's my answer.'

'Then you've answered the question.' By omitting the 'only' he had confirmed what Frankie already knew: that there was far more to this journey than he had disclosed, or was willing to disclose, to her.

'Well, then, your curiosity must be satisfied.' He looked down at her. 'You really are your father's daughter, aren't you? All these questions.'

'I like to know what's going on,' she admitted.

'Well, what's going on right now is that we carry on driving down into the plains so we can get well into the reserve and set up camp by nightfall.'

'Taking animal pictures isn't your normal style, though, is it?' she said, when they were driving once more along the dusty ribbon of road.

'Oh? And what's my normal style?'

'War,' she said. 'Famine. Earthquakes. Floods. Epidemics——'

'I take pictures of what I think is important, what I think people should know about.'

'And are animals important?'

'Yes, of course. In their own way.' He glanced at her. 'Although I'll admit this assignment is supposed to be a bit of a holiday. I've been working non-stop for months, and with this shoulder I can't do anything too strenuous.'

'Otherwise you'd be where? Angola? China?

Panama?' She plucked three headlines from television news bulletins.

'Probably.' He grinned. 'Probably all three. Do I scent disapproval?'

She shook her head. 'No. Only it's dangerous——'

'You don't have to tell me that. But someone has to do it, if you happen to believe that it's important that people know what's going on in the world, which I do. Just as your father did.'

'But Mike was always saying he was going to give it up. "Just one more story", he used to say, "just one more trip". And look what happened to him in the end!'

'He had a family; it was different for him.'

'You mean if you had a family you'd stop?'

'It's an entirely academic question. When you live out of a suitcase as I do, you tend not to give it much thought.'

She drove on in silence, remembering the newspaper cuttings she had read back in Yorkshire, and the documentary film she had watched.

'Penny for them.'

'What?' She was startled.

'I can feel that busy head of yours churning over.'

She swallowed. 'I was just wondering how much suffering one person could bear,' she said tentatively, 'without getting damaged by it in some way, hardened or bitter——'

'You think I'm hard and bitter?'

Yes, she thought. 'I don't know. You might be. I don't know anything about you.'

He shifted in his seat, pondering over her words, then he glanced over to her. 'If you must know, young

Frankie,' he said finally, 'it's a question I've been asking myself of late. When I find the answer, I'll let you know.'

The day passed in an endless trail of miles, but in the late afternoon they passed into the national park and began to see an abundance of game—zebra and buffalo and giraffe. Frankie stared around entranced, almost forgetting Cal by her side.

'It's wonderful!'

'Unfortunately rather a lot of other people think so, too.' He pointed across the plain to where a clutch of black and white striped safari vans was clustered in a circle round a tawny speck. 'The poor lions get no privacy any more. Let's make sure we're away from all that.' He read the map closely and directed her off on a side track and over a jumble of small broken hills. On the other side was a smaller plain, with no safari vehicles in sight.

'What about here?' He pointed to a lone thorn tree. 'It's flat, there's shade, and some useful branches to hang things on.'

'Can we just choose anywhere?' She switched off the engine and looked around. 'Aren't there special camping areas?'

'There are for most people, but we've got an exemption. The park authorities know what I'm doing.'

'Oh.' She got down. The landscape seemed vast. They were just tiny dots in the middle of infinity.

He got down and looked at her face. 'What's the matter? Did you expect running water and a cafeteria?'

'No, of course not.' She turned about. But she had somehow thought they would be camping near a game lodge, or with other campers on safari. Not in such complete and utter isolation.

Cal got busy and she joined in, working to his directions, until the camp was surprisingly organised and comfortable. There was the tent, a round fireplace of stones, a towel and tea-towels hanging from the thorns of the tree. Cal occupied himself with his camera equipment. She took his binoculars and climbed to the top of a small knoll to survey the scene. Even though the sun was setting, the rock still felt hot under her feet, and bright lizards scuttered away from her.

'Watch out for lions!' Cal called, squinting up at her. She pulled a face, but he said, 'I'm serious. You never know what's on the other side of a sunny rock out here.'

But there was nothing, and she sat for a long time training her field glasses on the scene until the peace and tranquillity of the plains seemed to fill her mind and her spirit.

Cal had vanished when she returned. She could make him out some distance away near a clump of bushes crouching, kneeling and stretching as he photographed something she could not see.

She watched his lithe figure move with grace and economy. It was obvious that he and his camera were one, and that when he was working he entirely forgot any pain his shoulder might give him.

The light was fading fast by the time he came back to her.

'What were you photographing?'

'Dung beetles. Nothing exciting. I'm just getting back in practice. Tomorrow I want you to drive me to a waterhole I've been told about. We'll make a dawn start. It might be a boring day for you.'

She shook her head. 'I could never be bored here! There's so much to watch.'

He took out a can of beer, opened it and drank. She watched him. He looked across at her, cursed softly under his breath, and got out another can for her.

'So you like Africa, do you, young Frankie O'Shea?'

'I love it. I knew I would.' She set her drink beside her and knelt to cut bread and slice tomatoes.

'It's like a mistress. Once you're under the spell you can't break free. Although I suppose in your case that should be "lover".'

Cal swigged reflectively on his beer, eyeing her speculatively, and she suddenly knew he was remembering how she had stood naked before him that morning. She battled with a blush, and won. 'It certainly beats London,' she said with feeling.

'You're not a city girl?'

'I don't know. I certainly didn't like it when I tried it, but maybe that was because of the job——'

'Ah, that sexual harassment again——'

'You can mock, but it was awful. And in the end it got frightening. He started making veiled threats.'

'So what did you do?'

'I walked out.'

'That's often the best way with problems. Turn your back on them and walk away.'

'Is that what you do?'

'It depends on the problem. If it's my own, I work it out; if it's a problem someone else is giving me, I prefer to just leave.'

'Love and leave,' she murmured, remembering what Alice had said.

'What?'

She looked up. 'It's your reputation—love and leave.'

'Newspaper rubbish,' he said scathingly. 'And anyway, my life doesn't allow much time for anything else.'

'But you can't just walk away from everyone who's giving you problems——'

'Can't you?'

'Well, look at my Aunt Jenny. I'm sure she would have liked to have turned her back on me hundreds of times. She was very happy living her quiet, spinsterly life, and then Mum was killed and Mike dumped me on her. And then he was killed, too, so she knew she was landed with me for life. And I don't suppose I was exactly easy to bring up. I was quite a tomboy, and wayward with it.'

'Like your father. Maybe you should follow in his footsteps and become a journalist.'

'No, I'm no good at words. I'm not good at anything very much. At the convent they said I had no application. But the lessons were all so boring!'

'You're a good driver. And a pretty good camp caterer.'

She dished out soup and fished jacket potatoes out of the fire.

'Useful skills in Skipton.'

'You'll find your niche. Give it time.'

'Oh, it's easy to say that when you've already found your own!'

'I was never without,' he admitted, sitting down and

reaching for the food. 'I knew what I wanted to do from the time I could walk. It was just a question of learning my craft.'

'And you said Mike helped you?' She looked at him eagerly. Cal seemed so much more affable out here in the bush that she longed to capitalise on his good humour. 'What did he seem like to you? Will you tell me about him?'

It was an innocent question, but she saw his head jerk up and his expression grow hard and closed. The bush had been silent as darkness settled, but now night noises began to pierce the quiet all around. She looked at him, surprised by the dark intensity of his look, and the way he deflected her question straight back to her. 'You must remember quite a lot about him yourself?'

'Oh, yes. I can remember him coming down the path to our front door, calling my name, with presents spilling out of every pocket. I loved his visits, they were magical times for me, and even Aunt Jenny used to get quite carried away. She'd drink three sherries and play the harmonium with gusto! But I never saw his serious side. I never saw him at work.'

Cal put down his plate, thinking carefully, and choosing his words slowly. 'He was a fine man, every-one thought so, and one of the best correspondents around. He knew everyone worth knowing, all kinds of doors were open to him, but he was never arrogant about his skills or his contacts.' He paused, then he looked up at Frankie, his eyes piercing in the firelight. 'He was very kind to me. I was just a young puppy when I first went out there, but he showed me patience and tolerance. I owed him everything, yet——' He stopped.

'Yet what?'

The night had suddenly grown twice as dark. Somewhere far off an animal howled.

There was a long silence. Then he said, 'Yet nothing.'

'You were going to go on.'

There was another long silence, then he began to talk swiftly, changing the subject. 'Let me tell you about a trip we once did out into the desert with a group of nomads, your father and I. We couldn't really talk to them because of the language barrier, but Mike poured them drinks and mimed jokes for them and you could see they loved him. Everyone did. He was one of those rare people who enhance people's lives. Everyone felt better for spending time with him.'

'His memorial service was crammed,' Frankie said. 'I had no idea he knew so many people.'

'I couldn't go. I was still in the Middle East. But I remember walking out of the hospital, into the garden, to be by myself at the time when it was happening. I thought about him, and how passionately I wished he was still alive.'

'Hospital?'

'It was nothing,' he said crisply.

She swallowed. 'Did you know how it happened— the bomb?' No one had ever told her more than the barest facts.

'Yes, I know.'

'What did happen?'

'It's enough that it happened,' he said, and his voice had grown hard and forbidding again. 'There's no point in dwelling on the details.' It was clear he would say no more.

'I felt so angry with him for getting killed,' she confessed. 'I couldn't cry because I felt so angry. In a way I still do. I feel I've missed so much by not knowing him now.'

'He would have still been abroad, in the Middle East, or somewhere. That was his life. There would always have been "one more trip".'

'I know, but he would have come back from time to time. I could have talked to him. Aunt Jenny just doesn't know what sort of person I am.'

'And do you, yet?'

He looked at her in the firelight and for a moment some sort of thread of invisible tension seemed to spin across the flames between them. Out here, alone in the vastness, they sat unmoving, held by the flickering light, until Frankie's heart began to bump uncomfortably round her ribs.

'I know enough. Enough to know that I could never stand the kind of future she had in mind for me.'

'Then you're halfway there, young Frankie.' He stood up, and away from the firelight he was only a dark silhouette, powerful and remote. 'You know what you don't want. Now you have to find out what you do.' And he walked away, swallowed up by the darkness, leaving her smarting at the way he had suddenly spoken down to her as if she were little more than a child.

Yet later that night she felt very much a child.

It was the early hours and something had woken her up. She sat bolt upright in her sleeping-bag, every sense aquiver, the hairs on her arms standing up on end. She was alone in the tent—Cal had chosen to take his sleeping-bag and sleep under the stars outside—but something was definitely moving close at hand.

'Oh!' She whimpered to herself as her ears strained in the darkness.

Somewhere, far off, there was a haunting chuckle which Cal had told her was a hyena, but it was not that which had scared her. She listened harder, holding her breath. Then it came again, a rasping, grunting noise so close to hand that it was almost in the tent. An animal was just the other side of the canvas and it could be anything—a lion or elephant or cheetah.

'Oh!' Her head whipped round. There it was again, but now from the other side. She was frozen with fear. The noise seemed to be all around her. Somewhere by her sleeping-bag there was a torch, but she was too scared to reach out her hand to it, too scared even to breathe.

Yet whatever was outside was breathing. She could hear hot animal breaths against the tent, then a dark shadow loomed up against the canvas.

'Oh!' She screamed, and the raw sound of her fear filled the air.

Within seconds the canvas flaps of her tent were being thrust aside.

'What in heaven's——?'

'Oh!' She fought to stifle another scream as she realised who it was. 'Oh, it's you!'

Suddenly her tension broke, and she began to tremble all over.

'There's something just outside—I don't know what. It woke me,' she got out. Now she was sobbing and shaking with fright.

Cal bent over and came in.

'Hey. Steady. Steady.' He knelt and put his arms round her, holding her hard until her shaking began to steady. He wore only shorts, and the warm skin of his arms and his chest soothed her fears. She leaned into his strength, still trembling against him like a terrified deer. 'Can't you hear it?'

He grinned. 'I can hear it. Look.' He put out an arm and lifted the tent flap and she slowly made out shapes dotting the grass 'It's a herd of wildebeest grazing their way past us. Nothing worse. They're noisy devils, but they'll do us no harm.'

Frankie looked at the animals scattered about the plain, as harmless as the sheep grazing in the field next to her Yorkshire home, and wanted to cry with humiliation and relief. 'Oh, I feel such a fool! I thought it was an elephant, at the very least.'

Cal spread his hands on her shoulders, holding her firmly so that she could feel his every finger on her flesh. 'All right now?' She looked at him, wide-eyed and tousled.

'I'm sorry. You must think I'm very stupid.'

His grey eyes looked into her green ones and as they did she saw them darken, and felt his mood shift.

'I woke you,' she burbled, unnerved by the change in him. 'And I'm behaving just like a girl——'

'The wildebeest had already woken me.'

He looked at her face, her neck, then down to where her body pushed against the thin cotton of her T-shirt, and she saw his throat move as his hands moved on her shoulders, moulding her slenderness, in the instinctive gesture of a sensual man. Her shaking had stopped, he could have let her go, but he did not. They seemed to kneel like that, facing each other, for minutes without speaking.

She looked up into his face, which was broodingly handsome in the dark shadows, and smelled the warmth of his skin, and a sudden, overwhelming desire for him arrowed through her. She closed her eyes against the assault on her senses. Was she crazy? She'd never felt like this before, not for any man, but the feeling was unmistakable. She wanted Cal, she wanted him as her lover, and she wanted him with a brute and primitive longing that almost propelled her hard into his arms.

She opened her eyes again, reeling inside from her feelings, and met Cal's steady gaze.

'What's the matter?' His voice was roughened. 'There's no danger.'

'I know,' she lied. But there was. The danger was here in the tent, beside her, inside her. And it was far more dangerous, far more wild, than any wild animal.

Their looks snagged, weighted with knowledge, and she felt her lips soften and part. His eyes went to her mouth.

'Do you want me to sleep in here for the rest of the night?'

Yes, said her body, yes; stay with me. No, said her common sense, no; you mustn't!

He dragged his eyes back to meet her gaze and at that moment something savage seemed to flare between them, as they both knew what would be the consequence of such a move.

'I——' she began, then stopped, her throat dry. She swallowed. 'No,' she got out, 'you mustn't.' She saw a movement in his throat as he, too, swallowed back his tension, then he slowly dropped his hands. 'No,' he said harshly, 'you're right. I mustn't.' And he went out, leaving her alone with her churning heart.

CHAPTER SIX

'PASS me my two hundred mill. lens,' Cal murmured quietly.

Frankie picked it deftly out of his camera-case and passed it over, then kept her hand outstretched, ready to take the lens he was removing from his camera out of his grasp. A cow elephant, with a baby, was coming slowly out of the bushes on the other side of the water. She watched the two animals step to the water's edge, dainty despite their huge feet, and watched Cal shoot them unerringly with the harmless trigger of his camera.

They crouched together in the scrub near the Land Rover. Cal lowered his camera and waited. He wore khaki shorts and a T-shirt. Sweat slicked his bronzed shoulders and ran down his face.

She looked at him, then quickly away, not daring to let her gaze linger. When she did, her throat seemed to close until she could scarcely breathe. On a branch near by was a beautiful bird, vivid with blue and lavender plumage, and she distracted herself by concentrating on it.

Cal, sensing her fascination with his work, had loaned her one of his cameras and now she raised it from where it hung round her neck and focused it on the bird. She clicked the trigger just as it rose from the branch, and hoped she had captured the beauty of its sunlit take-off.

Cal looked round at the sound and their eyes met. Then he, too, looked away.

'Oh!'

She let her breath out in a stifled sigh of need and longing. They were so close, their bare legs almost touching, and yet they were so far apart. She was acutely aware of his every breath and movement, and she felt sure he was of hers. And yet how could she be so sure? Nothing had been said, nothing had been spoken. All there was between them were these uncomfortable, jarring looks, the vibrations of their bodies, and the way her very blood seemed to beat for him.

It was the fourth day of their trip. Four long, sunny days when they had risen at dawn and slept at nightfall, and had spent the hours in between driving and watching, waiting and working.

In some ways they had been the best days of her life. She had felt alive and free, and had loved learning about the wildlife of the African bush. She had also found a new thrill, she thought, resting her hand on the hot metal of the camera, because from watching Cal and asking him questions about photography she had quickly picked up the basic technicalities of his craft and was enjoying the chance to put her new knowledge into practice. She had no idea if her pictures would be good, but Cal was a patient teacher, and she certainly enjoyed learning from him.

But in other ways they had been by far the worst. Ever since that first night, when Cal had come to her and taken her into his arms, a whole new and distinctly uncomfortable element had entered their relationship. Sexual tension simmered and throbbed just below the surface of their every exchange, and seemed to grow more powerful by the day. Whether it was their fingers touching as she passed him a camera lens, or his eyes resting darkly on her slender legs, there was a quality to their awareness of each other that permeated every movement and made her ache with raw desire. And she was somehow sure he felt the same.

Although it could never be the same, she thought bitterly. Because while she had never known before what a powerful and driving force desire could be, Cal, she was certain, felt only the familiar arousal of a passing interest.

She sensed his eyes on her face and flicked her green gaze to his.

'What is it?'

'What are you thinking about? You're frowning like an angry polecat.'

I was thinking about all the women you must have taken to bed in your roving life, she thought. 'I was thinking how frustrating it must be for you to have to have an assistant, when you're so used to travelling alone.'

'Frustrating.' His mouth crooked with cool irony. 'I'd say that was the right word.' For a moment his eyes stayed on her, watching as her blush deepened beneath his gaze, then he looked down to his camera. She saw the dark fan of his eyelashes on his bronzed skin as he twisted off the camera lens and put it carefully back in his bag.

'It has its drawbacks,' he said, in a brisker voice, 'but I'll say something for you, Frankie, you're a damn fine photographic assistant. I've never known anyone pick it up so quickly.'

Her blush turned to a glow of pleasure. 'I'm fascinated by it. I love watching you work. You're teaching me so much.'

'Yes, well——' He got up and bent to place his cameras in the bag. Then he stopped, one camera still weighed in his hand, and looked directly down at her. She saw his straight brown fingers on the black metal, and knew before he began to speak that he was going to break the unwritten silence that had bound them during the past few days.

'—let's keep it to photography, shall we? Then neither of us will run into trouble.'

There was a silence so deep that she could hear the rustle of the breeze in the grasses of the plain.

'I don't know what you mean!'

'Oh, yes you do. You might be young—but you're not that young.'

Frankie looked down, unable to meet his eyes. Her gaze rested on his hands, strong and sensitive. Her cheeks felt on fire. She heard him sigh with irritation, and imagined him pushing a hand through his hair. The heat seemed to press all round them.

'You know how things are, you know as well as I do. But I'm telling you straight, it's going no further. You're young and innocent. I'm not. You can't even begin to imagine what my life has been like——'

'Can anyone?' Her green gaze blazed up at him. 'If I was twice as old, would it make any difference? Anyway, I don't see what all this has to do with anything!'

'It has to do with the fact that, whatever's started to happen between us, there is no way whatsoever we're going to do anything about it! For one thing,' he added cruelly, 'convent girls have never been my style.'

'How many times do I have to tell you? I'm not a convent girl! Although I rather thought that any and every woman was grist for your mill!'

'On the contrary, I'm extremely selective. I've just been lucky enough to have had a rich and varied field to choose from.'

'Oh!' she cried out with distaste. 'Anyway, I wasn't intending to do anything about anything!'

'I know. Look. . .' He put out a conciliatory hand and touched her arm, flesh on flesh. She drew back as if he'd burned her. 'I know you can't help looking like you do, and smiling like you do, but——'

'But you never wanted to take a girl on this trip in the first place, and now all your worst nightmares have come to pass!' She jumped up, dusting down her shorts. 'OK. Fine. You were right and I was wrong—but there's not much we can do about it now, is there, except grin and bear it?'

'We can at least air the problem. If we don't, it'll be like a pressure-cooker building up steam. One day it— we'll—explode!'

'OK. It's aired.'

'You're angry now, but you'll understand when——'

Frankie raised her eyes in exasperation. 'I know! Don't tell me! When I'm older. Well, I'm not exactly a babe in arms, you know!'

'But you haven't exactly seen a lot of life yet, have you? Being incarcerated in a convent for ten years doesn't give you much to go on.'

She glared at him. 'You know what? I think you

need to keep casting me as a convent schoolgirl for your own protection. Otherwise you might have to start seeing me as a real person, and that would never do, would it?'

'I do see you as a real person. Far too real. That's the problem.' Cal dashed a hand through his hair. His look was grim. 'For God's sake, Frankie, I'm trying to do the decent thing, for once in my life. I don't see why you have to get so damned angry about it!'

'I'll tell you why! It's because I feel you're accusing me of having done something, but I don't know what it is! I've tried my utmost to do everything you've asked, to stay out of your hair, and not get in your way—I've hardly been prancing around in a basque and suspenders, holding out an apple and trying to lure you away from your cameras and into the undergrowth!'

He looked up at her, dragging an arm across his brow to wipe away the sweat. She saw a sudden wicked glint in his eyes under the shadow of his arm. 'The trouble is that khaki shorts are far more sexy on the right woman——'

'Well, that's your problem, not mine!' she snapped, furious. 'If you expect me to start donning a *chador* in this weather, then you're in for a disappointment. I'm dressing for comfort, and to hell with what effect it has on anyone else!'

'Ah, the famous O'Shea temper. I wondered if you'd inherited that, too!'

He looked away, then back at her. She saw his eyes straying to the way her breasts pushed out the thin white cotton of her T-shirt, and her tiny waist clinched with a brown leather belt. His look was dark with desire and his lips were parted, showing a dangerous edge of straight teeth. At the sight of him her heart seemed to somersault over, turn to water, and melt clean away. She moistened her lips, and he watched her.

'If it were only different——' he said roughly.

'If pigs could fly!'

He sighed. 'Maybe this conversation wasn't such a brilliant idea, but it's too late to worry now. We both know the score. The least we can do is try and make things easy for each other. OK?'

It might be easy for you, she thought bitterly, but it would never be easy for her, not when she only had to see the curve of his mouth or the plane of his cheek to feel almost faint with raw desire.

'All right,' she said sullenly.

'Good girl,' he said, and walked away as if the matter had dropped instantly from his mind. Across the water-hole the elephant mother and her baby were retreating into the bush. He stopped and watched them, hands on his hips.

'The sun's getting high now. We won't see much game for the rest of the day.'

He glanced back, and she tore her eyes from the strong lines of his body and pretended to be studying the scene.

'I got some good pictures of those two,' he said. 'The only thing I haven't got now is a cheetah.'

'Are they rare?'

'They're shy. Elusive quarry.' He looked at her and their eyes met, and it was as if his words had nothing whatsoever to do with wild animals and everything in the world to do with her. Desire, refusing to be banished, flared between them again. She caught up her lip under his gaze, and his eyes darkened.

'Oh, hell and damnation! This is utterly impossible!' He turned abruptly. 'Did you bring breakfast?'

'Don't I always?'

She marched to the Land Rover, not knowing whether she was more furious with him for the way he was so coolly rejecting her, or with herself for showing him her feelings so nakedly.

'Cheers.' He eyed her over the rim of his mug. 'You know, you make great coffee.'

'You don't have to humour me!'

'I wasn't. I was making a simple observation.'

'Well, thank you. At least I'm good for something.'

Her words snapped his temper. He turned and hit the Land Rover hard with his fist, making her jump with shock. 'For God's sake, quit this martyr act! You're good for a million things, and you know it! You're just not good for me!'

Their eyes blazed at each other. Frankie turned, leaned her arms up against the side of the vehicle, and rested her forehead against them. 'I didn't mean it to be like this,' she said miserably.

'Neither did I. And even if it was, I thought I could handle it.'

'And you can.' The bitterness was still in her tone.

There was a long silence. Then Cal said harshly. 'I *have* to. I have no option. But I'll tell you straight, it's one hell of a struggle.'

She swallowed, then spoke in a muffled rush into her arms. 'Who says you have to?'

There was a long, long silence. Her words seemed to hang shimmering in the hot air. She could hear them echoing in her ears, and she could hardly believe what she heard. Had she really said that? She, who had always been so cool and in control with the few boyfriends she had allowed to court her; she, whose experience of hot-breathed bosses had made her as wary as any wild creature of flirtatious games and light-hearted dalliances?

But this wasn't a game, it was real, more real than anything she had ever felt before. And, driven by her wild feelings, she had allowed the raw abandon that tore at her heart to be mirrored plainly in her shameless, blurted words.

She held her breath. She heard him sigh, and when he finally spoke it was with careful emphasis.

'I'm not sure I heard that right,' she heard him say, 'but I can make an educated guess. And the answer is, because I just do.'

'You mean there's someone else?' She looked up, but his eyes scowled away into the distance.

'I didn't say that,' he said, after a moment. 'But look at you, Frankie. You're so innocent and open to the world that you make me feel a hundred. I've no right to take that from you, no intention of doing so——'

She flung her head back, tossing her hair, and looked him straight in the eyes. 'Twenty isn't so young. And innocence can't last forever.'

'You're a very young twenty.'

'All the more reason to do some catching up!'

'For God's sake, what are you saying? You want to use me to lose your virginity? You want me to give you a taste of experience?'

'No, no! I don't mean that! I don't know what I

mean!' Spelt out so baldly, the words frightened her, made her back away. 'You're twisting everything up!'

'Exactly. You don't know what you mean. You don't know what you want. But let me tell you something. We're in a hothouse out here—together night and day, cut off from the outside world. It's not the sort of situation for a little light dalliance. You might want me to hold you, kiss you. But just suppose I did? Where do you think we would end up?'

Frankie met his eyes and saw a ruthless honesty there that humbled her and made her ashamed of her blundering outcries.

'In bed. Or rather in sleeping-bag.' Her lips crooked miserably.

'And is that what you really, honestly want?'

'I don't know.' Somewhere, out of the far corner of her eye, she seemed to see the dim outline of her aunt Jenny's worried face. 'I just can't stand things the way they are.'

'That's a "no". And you don't have to stand things much longer. Tonight we're going to drive over to the Mana Lodge. I've got to go away for a couple of days, and I want you to stay there while I'm gone.'

'What?' She was aghast. 'Go away? Why?'

'There's some pictures I have to take.'

'But you can't go alone. You can't drive.'

'I can manage.'

'How? Who with? Where are you going?' She felt herself go cold, bereft and spurned.

'I can't tell you now. If everything goes well, I'll explain when I get back.'

'Is it dangerous?'

'Crossing a road's dangerous.'

'That's a "yes"!'

He dashed a hand through his hair.

'Why can't I come?'

'Because I don't want you with me,' he said cruelly. 'I don't want anyone with me.'

'Oh!'

'I'm sorry, but it's how things have to be.'

'And what about the International Wildlife budget? Can it suddenly stretch to luxury game lodges?'

'This is not their job, it's mine. And my budget. And,' he added grimly, 'this time it extends to two rooms when we're both there together. I'm not risking those seductive pyjamas of yours any more.'

'I haven't got them with me.' She managed a bleak smile. 'I left them in my case, back in Nairobi. It's a T-shirt or my birthday suit.'

'Even more reason,' he said gravely. 'Come on, let's go. I've got a hundred things to do back at camp.'

CHAPTER SEVEN

'HOLD it.' Cal's voice was tense. 'We have visitors.'

It had been a hot and silent drive back to camp, but now Cal leaned forward and spoke urgently. Frankie looked up from the bumpy track she had been guiding the Land Rover along, and saw a vehicle parked near their distant tent. He put out a hand and pressured her thigh in silent signal to stop. His fingers on her bare skin were not in the slightest bit sensual, and his eyes were glued to the scene ahead. Suddenly he was as watchful as a poised hawk, quivering and alert. She could almost feel the adrenalin beginning to pulse through his veins.

'What is it?'

'I don't know.'

'It must just be game wardens or something. After all, we aren't doing anything wrong.'

'It isn't that simple.' He glanced behind them. 'Back up. See if we can get behind those thorn bushes. But for God's sake don't roar the engine.'

Trembling, she did as she was told, but before they could reach shelter there was a shout, and then the vehicle near their tent burst into life and drove wildly across the plain towards them, setting up a cloud of dust.

Cal swore violently under his breath.

'What is it? What's happening?'

'I'm not sure, but it doesn't look good.

Frankie——' His eyes snapped to hers. 'Whatever happens now, do whatever I say. Do you hear that? Whatever. And leave me to do all the talking.'

His tone brooked no questioning. She nodded, her heart pounding.

'Trust me,' he said, his eyes compelling hers, and then there was no more time for talking because the vehicle, which she could now see was an ancient, open-topped lorry, was bearing down on them fast, and in the back she could see a group of wild-eyed men waving their fists in the air.

No, not fists, she realised with a sickening lurch of fear. Guns.

Cal got out and stood in their path, his hands away from his sides as if to prove his own unarmed status. The lorry slowed to a dusty halt. There was a lot of shouting in an African language she did not understand, then two men stepped forward, grabbed Cal, and strong-armed him into the back of the lorry.

'Cal!'

Her cry made the men turn. One came over and pulled her roughly down from her seat.

'Ow!' She stumbled, regained her balance, and pulled her arm free. 'I'm coming. You don't have to do that.'

To her astonishment, now that she was actually face to face with these hostile strangers, her fear fled and left her with an icy calm. When they shouted in her face she coolly walked to the lorry and climbed aboard next to Cal.

'Charming friends you have,' she muttered, as she took her place next to him on the grimy floor.

'They're no friends of mine,' he muttered back

grimly, his eyes flicking everywhere at once as he tried to take in exactly what was happening.

Then the man who seemed to be the group's leader vaulted into the back of the lorry and poked her roughly with the muzzle of his gun, shouting a single word over and over again.

'Keys,' said Cal. 'He wants the Land Rover keys.'

Her eyes flew to his.

'Give them to him.'

She stood up, felt in the pocket of her shorts, and handed them over. The man departed, and a moment or two later she heard the jeep start up and depart.

'Your cameras! Your films!' she gasped to Cal, but he only shushed her with his hand, and then the lorry roared into life and they were bumping so painfully across the bush that she could not think of anything but the bruising agony of the journey.

The rattling nightmare went on and on until she thought she could bear it no longer. It threw her and Cal constantly against each other, then apart, like helpless rag-dolls, and after a time it felt as if every part of her body was on fire with pain.

'Ouch!' she yelped as a particularly bad bump knocked her head against the iron side of the lorry. She glared at the men who were standing guard over them. 'Lousy driver you've got!'

One of the men snarled and muttered, levelling his gun towards her. Cal instantly flung an arm across her body to hold her still.

'Easy. Don't panic.'

'I wasn't planning to,' she said through clenched teeth, and it was true. She felt raw with pain and cold with fury, but not in the slightest bit panicky.

Cal looked at her. 'Why, I believe you're right,' he muttered, over the roar of the lorry.

'Of course I'm right!' His gaze, though dark, was immensely comforting, and she realised suddenly that it was because of him, and his steadfast presence beside her, that she had no fear.

Cal raised his voice and talked at length to the man, who eventually lowered his gun with a grunt.

'What's that language? What did you say?'

'What?'

The grinding of gears cancelled out all other noise. He bent his head and she shouted her questions again, her lips against his ear.

'It's Swahili.'

'And what did you say.'

His eyes glinted at her. 'A little white lie.'

'What sort of white lie?'

He hesitated. Then he bent his head towards hers. 'I told him my wife was expecting a child, and that she was frightened the bumping would damage the baby. That was why she cried out.'

She almost laughed. 'I certainly feel sick enough.'

He moved stiffly and put his arm around her. 'Here, we'd better give the story some credibility.'

His embrace cushioned the worst of the bumps and comforted her with human warmth.

'Oh, that's better.'

'Even so, I'd cut down on the wisecracks if I were you. I doubt if they intend to shoot us, but I wouldn't say these boys are the most safety-conscious marksmen around.'

'Who are they, anyway?'

The roar of the ancient engine was terrible. He could not hear her.

'What?'

'Who are they——? Oh, never mind!' She shrugged at Cal, then leaned back against him, defeated.

To her amazement the endless jolting must have hypnotised her into sleep, because when she opened her eyes the lorry was slowing to a halt and the sky was darkening. She straightened her head up from where it had been resting against Cal's shoulder.

'Where are we? What's happening?'

'Shush. Just wait and see.'

The lorry bumped to a merciful halt and the men jumped out and signalled to them to follow. Cal leapt down with agility, but she was stiff from sleep and fell awkwardly into his arms as he turned to help her.

The familiar male smell of him washed over her as he caught her up, and she grimaced at the irony of their sudden, enforced togetherness after their painful conflict that morning.

Yet this morning could have been a lifetime away, she thought, and Cal's proximity now no longer meant desperate desire, but strength and warmth and hope.

'OK now?'

'Yes, just pins and needles.'

'You're doing fine.'

His approval warmed her.

'Better than at word processing, anyway.'

She saw the gleam of his teeth as he grinned at her resilience, and was glad she had managed to sound perky, even though she did not feel it. Cold and hunger were beginning to sap her spirit, but she did not want Cal to see. She knew he had enough to handle without needing to worry about his unwanted girl companion having a nervous collapse at his side.

She could see in the rapidly darkening sunset that they were still way out in the middle of the deserted bush. The place where they had stopped was simply a ramshackle camp with two tattered canvas tents and a litter of empty bottles and cans.

'Not too hot on housekeeping,' she observed, wrinkling her nose. 'Or manners,' she added, as a gun was poked in her back and she was pushed towards one of the two tents.

Cal was pushed in after her, and the flaps pulled down so that they were sitting in a stifling blackness.

There was a silence.

'Wildlife photography,' she snorted disparagingly, after a time. 'I suppose this is the "associated game park activity"!'

'Wait.'

She heard a tiny sawing sound and then a fragment of light and air entered the tent.

'Swiss army knife,' Cal explained. 'It was in my shorts pocket. Like your father, I never travel without one.'

She could see his profile now, dark and strong, as he surveyed the scene through the tiny spy-hole he had made.

'Aren't you going to tell me who they are?'

'Shush. I'm thinking.'

'Oh!' She eyed him savagely. 'You've had hours to do that.'

'I didn't know where they were taking us, then.'

'And you do now. So do I. The middle of nowhere.'

'There's six of them altogether,' he said, looking out.

'Great. You take the left-hand three, I'll take the right——'

'Frankie, please——'

'Well, what do you want me to do? Sit down and wail? I could easily, you know.' Her voice rose with a waver. The thick darkness of the tent was far more oppressive than being in the lorry, and the hopelessness of their situation was beginning to overwhelm her.

The silence told her he was weighing up whether to relent or not.

'It would just help me,' she said tersely, 'to know why we're here. At the moment it makes no sense at all.'

'All right. These men are poachers. If they are who I think they are, they've been ravaging this area for years. There's a high price on their heads.' His words rattled out like machine-gun fire. 'I had a tip-off that they were about to mount a major operation in an area near where we were camping. I was hoping to go out and catch them at their tricks. That's why I was going to put you in the Mana Lodge for a couple of nights. But they got to me before I got to them.'

'Ivory poachers?'

'Mainly. But anything else, too, that gets in their path.'

'Ugh.' Frankie shook her head. 'But how did they know about you?'

'I guess my informant decided that a two-way tip-off was more profitable than a one-way one. . .'

'And now what?' The whites of her eyes showed in the darkness.

'I don't know exactly. But I doubt if they'd do anything really drastic. They're shrewd enough to realise what the consequences would be. My hunch is they want to get me out of the area, and to scare the living daylights out of me at the same time so that I won't come back another day.'

'What about the Land Rover? And your cameras?'

'I don't know. Ah——' He bent down and peered at the hole. 'Here's the Land Rover, at any rate. Good.' He looked back at her. 'If their leader's here, these men are less likely to get any silly notions——'

'About——?'

'About anything. Me—or you.'

'Oh.' Cal heard the sudden jolt of fear in Frankie's voice.

'I won't let them lay a finger on you!'

'There's six of them——'

'Then it's time for brain, not brawn.' He stood up.

'Where are you going?' she cried sharply.

'To parley. While it's still light enough to read their expressions. Don't worry, I'll be back.'

A long time later he returned, his breath smelling of whisky.

'Just popped out for a drink?'

'I'm bushed, Frankie. Cut the crummy jokes.'

She could hear from the strain in his voice that it was no time for the kind of brittle humour she was using to keep her spirits up. She fell silent.

'I've been talking. Bartering.'

'What for?'

'Our freedom. I wouldn't say it was the greatest deal ever struck, but it was the best I could do. In exchange for the Land Rover, all my camera equipment, and my solemn word that we will keep silent about ever having seen this gang, we will get driven out of here tomorrow morning and dumped somewhere within striking distance of a road.'

'Oh.' She contemplated what he had said. 'Well, at least if we're near a road——'

'I'm afraid a road round here means any sandy track that might see one vehicle a year.'

'Ah.'

'It doesn't look good, does it?'

'No.'

He sighed heavily. 'I'm sorry. I should never have got you into this mess.'

'No! I'm the one who should be sorry—sorry you've got to worry about me, as well as yourself. . .'

'You're doing wonderfully,' he said quietly. 'Better than I would ever have imagined. I'd take my hat off to you, if I had one.' For a moment they eyed each other silently in the darkness. 'Anyway,' he went on briskly, 'it could work out better than it looks, if things go according to plan. I sealed the deal with a couple of bottles of Scotch I had tucked away under the back seat of the Land Rover, and if my hunch is correct they'll all be totally blotto by midnight.'

'You mean we could get away then?'

'Uh-uh.' He shook his head. 'We wouldn't get very far in the dark. We'd probably drive in a circle and end up back here.'

'Anyway——' Frankie's spirits sank '—they've got the Land Rover keys.'

'Had the keys.' There was a chink of metal. 'While I was groping around inside for the whisky, in the dark, I managed to get hold of the set of house-keys that were in my jacket-pocket. The lad guarding me wasn't very bright. I locked the door with the proper keys, then handed him the other set. He didn't seem to notice any difference. So he's now the proud owner of the front-door key to Number Five, Regency Place, London, and—as far as I can remember—a room key to the Majestic Hotel, Singapore!'

'I can't see him very much at home there,' Frankie said, remembering the gloomy grey room overlooking the park.

'The Majestic?'

'No. Number Five, Regency Place.'

'Well, that would make two of us.'

'But it's your home!'

'House. More of an office than a home. I give Elaine a pretty free hand to indulge her taste for opulent gloom.'

'And don't you care?'

'I'm never there. And when I am, I'm either too busy or too dog-tired to notice.'

She thought about that.

'Cal?'

'Yes?'

Unconsciously they were both talking in low, intimate voices. 'I don't understand you. Why you live like you do. Why you keep putting yourself on the line like this. You must get to the end of your tether?'

'Of course I do. I'm only human, like everyone else.' He fell silent. 'As to the rest of it, I could answer that in a lot of ways. On good days I'd tell you I enjoy it. On bad——'

'What?'

'I don't know, I'd probably say it's just a habit.'

'Anyway,' she said, following her own thoughts, 'I suppose it has its advantages.'

'What do you mean?'

'Well, it's quite a convenient lifestyle in some ways, isn't it? If anything gets too tough, or too close, or too permanent, you just pack your bags and move on.' Her voice twisted with a bitterness that surprised her. 'Mike was the same. He hated the kind of everyday responsibilities other people took for granted. He loved buying me presents, but he never once bought me a birthday present. It was just too much effort to remember the date, to go out and buy something in time, to wrap it up and post it off to me.'

'That's as may be, but I'm not Mike.' Cal's voice sharpened in response to her tone. 'And I really don't want to be blamed for his parental inadequacies. After all, I don't have anyone back home I have to feel responsible for.'

'And never will,' she said flatly.

So that was the source of her bitterness, she realised suddenly. The certain knowledge that she would never get close to Cal—that no one would. He was a born and bred loner, tough and self-sufficient, and would always stay that way.

'I don't know about that. I'm not a clairvoyant. Anyway,' his tone lightened, 'you forget, as far as our dear custodians are concerned, I already have a wife and family in tow.'

'Oh, yes. My latest role in a long line of starring parts——' Frankie grimaced as she spoke, but he put up a warning hand.

'Don't start that all over again. I said it for your own protection. According to their beliefs, as a pregnant wife you're due some respect. As a single woman travelling unchaperoned in the bush with a man you're little better than a bar girl in their eyes.'

'I wasn't going to argue. I understood why you said it.' She closed her eyes. What would it be like to be Cal's wife, expecting his child? It was unimaginable. He was so cold and remote. Yet at the same time she felt warmed and reassured by his presence. He radiated such strength that she only had to glance at him to feel her fear die down in the face of his calm resourcefulness.

A burst of raucous laughter from the camp-fire made them both jump. 'It seems to be working,' said Cal, peering out. 'Our guard's gone to join the merry band.'

'Thank goodness!'

'I'll rest easier when they've drunk themselves to a standstill. Come here.'

'What?' For a moment she thought she was hearing things.

'We ought to get some sleep if we're to have our wits about us later,' he explained. 'And I want you away from the doors on this side of me. That way, if anyone decides to come visiting, they'll have to contend with me first.'

'Oh, I see.'

Gingerly she stepped over him and lay down on the groundsheet. It felt clammy beneath her bare legs and arms, and she shivered. 'They might have given us blankets.'

'And food,' he pointed out, 'and water. And soap and towels. But unfortunately they're not the type. Thank goodness we're only staying in this hotel for one night.'

She giggled. 'You really don't mind too much, do you? It's just another day in your life.'

'I wouldn't say you're exactly falling to pieces, either. I'd guess there's a little bit of the O'Shea in you that half enjoys a touch of drama and excitement.'

'A touch, maybe, but not this much. If I let myself dwell on the fix we're in, then I'm absolutely petrified. I can only cope as long as I don't think.'

'Then sleep is obviously the best solution.' She heard him stretch out at her back, then groan. 'I see what you mean. It's freezing.'

She hugged herself with her arms, but it made no difference. She heard him move irritably, this way and that. They were so close that she could feel a faint heat from his body, and their proximity made her catch her breath. Desire had died away in the face of danger and disaster, but now its dull, insistent tattoo began to drum dimly again in her veins.

How well she knew him, she thought. They had been together night and day for days, and she had absorbed his every mood and expression. She knew the humped outline of his sleeping figure at night, and the way he stooped and peered into the Land Rover's mirror to shave in the morning. She knew the strong lines of his limbs, and the spring of the dark hair that covered them. She knew how his hair curved into his neck, and how his eyes could glint dangerously with anger and desire.

Yet she knew nothing about him, nothing at all. She could not begin to guess at his thoughts, as he lay there beside her. All she knew was that no man had ever enthralled her and enraged her as he did; no man had ever disturbed her so much, yet given her so much peace.

'Cal?' Her thoughts turned restlessly.

'Yes.'

'How will we be sure to wake up in time?'

'Don't worry. That's not a problem. Getting to sleep, on the other hand, might be——'

'I know.' Her teeth chattered. She heard him sigh.

Then he said, 'I guess you'd better come here,' and his hand was on her arm, easing her back into the curve of his body. The moment he did so, it seemed the only possible thing to do. She curled unresisting into his warmth like a cat by the fire. She could feel his legs, hips, chest against hers, and his arms went firmly around her, holding her close.

'Since you're my wife——' he murmured against her neck, and her blood pounded at the softness of his breath against her ear. But he did not allow his lips to brush her neck, or his hands to stroke her arms, and within minutes, it seemed to her, he was soundly asleep.

Much, much later she, too, finally managed to force her restless body into a sleep which, surprisingly, was broken only once when Cal shifted abruptly, next to her. She woke up and knew immediately why. In sleep, his hand had strayed to cup her breast and his body had hardened with repressed desire until, waking, he had pulled himself sharply away from her. She felt the lonely ache he had aroused in her and longed to turn into his arms and feel the force of his embrace again. But she willed herself not to. Just as he had shown her dignity and restraint under these most difficult circumstances, so she, too, struggled to give him the space and privacy that he so clearly wanted. And eventually, despite her troubled thoughts, she succeeded, and drifted off into a light, troubled sleep once again.

CHAPTER EIGHT

'RIGHT. Come on, let's go,' Cal hissed.

In the first glimmer of dawn they skirted the sprawled, comotose bodies of their captors, and made for the Land Rover. Frankie's heart was pounding fit to burst, but Cal's firm grip on her hand steadied her. When they reached the jeep he let her go and turned to unlock the door.

She looked back at the scene around the still-smouldering fire. Something caught her eye. Without thought, she darted quickly forward and, fleet-footed as a deer, sped silently across the camp-site.

Cal was black with fury when she returned.

'What in hell do you think you were doing? They could wake at any moment!'

'Don't ask! Just drive,' she gasped, throwing herself in beside him.

The engine burst into life with an exploding splutter that could have woken up the dead, but none of the men stirred. Cal eased out on to the track, then accelerated as fast as he dared. She looked back. No one was coming after them. She looked in front. In the thin, dawn light, the plains were grey and silent.

'We did it!'

'Don't be so sure. They could easily catch us up in that tank of theirs.'

His voice told her he was still angry. She looked at him and saw his face, hard and dark. Then he grimaced as the vehicle lurched in a rut of sand and jolted his damaged shoulder.

'I should be driving, not you!'

'You're damn lucky to be here at all. I should have gone without you—What were you doing? Collecting souvenirs?'

'No. Your camera bag.'

He looked across, surprised, but unbending. 'It's all insured. It wasn't worth the risk.'

'There were your films, too.'

'I could have shot them again.'

'Well, my films, then,' she said with asperity. 'They were the first pictures I've ever taken. I wasn't going to lose them, if I could help it!'

Her tone made him relent, then laugh.

'You've really got the bug, haven't you?'

'I don't know. I think so. It depends if they're any good.'

'I'll be surprised if they're not,' he said, and he shot her a quick glance. 'You've got a good eye. And passion and dedication. All the makings of a good photographer.'

Passion, she thought, remembering the embrace of his aroused body in the night, and looking at him, and the way his smile warmed his whole handsome face, her heart grew huge and sore.

'It all depends what you want,' he said.

I want you, she answered silently to herself. That's all I want. I want you, and I want you to love me! The word startled her. Love. Love and Cal didn't seem at all compatible. She still stared at him with wide eyes. He might make love to women, he might love and leave, but real love—why, he had always made plain that such commitment and permanence had no place in his life.

She swallowed down a painful lump. Cal glanced from the road, back to her.

'What is it?'

'Nothing.'

She stared miserably ahead. Falling in love with Cal Fenton was probably the most stupid thing any woman could do. It certainly hadn't been part of her plan. But it had happened, she suddenly realised, and there wasn't a single, solitary thing she could do to change the situation.

Silent, each locked in his own thoughts, they drove until the sun came up, warming the landscape with a golden glow. Herds of gazelles grazed peacefully, and the birds chirruped their morning chorus.

'I think we're OK now. Let's stop and have a beer. It's not much of a breakfast, but I think that's all there is.'

Cal slowed to a halt. They got out into the fresh morning air. The sun was warm on Frankie's arms, driving away the chill of exhaustion and hunger. She looked around, and to her horror she felt tears springing to her eyes. Everything around them was so beautiful and at peace, yet inside she was a raging mass of unfulfilled dreams and hopeless longings. Even worse, the tears, once started, would not stop. They spilled down her cheeks and splashed on to her dusty T-shirt until she was gulping and sobbing without restraint.

'Hey!' Cal, rooting for the beers, looked up at the sound. Then he was by her side, catching her close, holding her hard to him. 'Easy, Frankie, easy.' His hands roamed her back and hair, soothing her as he might a frightened child. 'It's over now. Everything's OK. It's all finished.'

'I don't know what's the matter,' she gasped out, shaking in his arms. Her tears seemed to come from some bottomless pit, as if she was crying not just for the moment, but for all the losses and failures she had ever known.

Cal pushed the hair from her wet face, stroking it behind her ears. 'It's delayed shock, and exhaustion. It's a perfectly normal reaction.'

She shook her head, her eyes meeting his. 'I'm not frightened. I'm—I don't know what I am——'

He looked deep into her gaze.

'Well, I do. You're beautiful, and brave, and honest——' He stopped, and swallowed.

For a long moment their looks snagged so nakedly that she was sure he must bend his head and take her lips with his. The current flowing between their bodies was electric, a pulse of awareness that drove the blood faster through her veins and made her half dizzy with desire. Then, just as she thought something must happen or she would die from the tension, his voice toughened purposefully. 'And I certainly know one thing: your father would have been very proud of you,' and he set her deliberately away from him.

She turned her back on him, desolated by his restraint and rigid self-control.

'Nothing seems to affect you!' she cried bitterly.

'Oh, you'd be surprised.' There was an edge of iron in his voice.

'You don't get frightened! You don't lie awake at night! You don't let anyone get close to you!'

'What if I'm just a damn good actor?' She turned back and saw a blaze of anger in his eyes.

'Then why bother to act?' she blazed. 'Why waste all that effort? What's the point? Unless it's to fool yourself.'

'The point is, it wouldn't help to have two of us scared out of our wits, or sobbing our hearts out, or——'

'Or what?' Frankie scorned, blind with anger.

'Or you know what!' He dashed his hand through his hair. 'You know damned well what! My God, Frankie, you try my patience! For two pins I'd up-end you and give you a good hiding!'

'So that's how you get your kicks!'

'Why, you little madam!'

His eyes narrowed dangerously and he stepped forward, gripping her shoulders with fingers that bit so hard into her flesh that she cried out.

'Ow! You're hurting!'

'People who provoke must live with the consequences,' he gritted, and his eyes were a battleground of dark emotions, and his expression was ruthless.

Frankie's heart stopped, but her spirit rose up to lock with his. 'Have you ever seen me running away?' she challenged him.

His look glittered, then, with a rough growl of impatience, his mouth came down on hers with a harsh, hurting urgency that bruised her lips and forced her head back hard against the side of the Land Rover. His body pressed against hers, and she felt his desire flame instantly.

It was what she had longed for, had ached for, yet now it was all wrong—far too much, far too soon—

and in her fragile state his brutal need frightened her and made her quail.

Almost immediately he pulled away from her, his breath rasping harshly, but his hand still clasped her hair at the base of her neck.

'How much do you even know about men, Frankie? Oh, not teenage boyfriends or elderly bosses who try to paw your knee, but real men? What they feel? What they need?'

She looked at him with wide, shocked eyes.

'Nothing, I'll bet?'

She shook her head dumbly.

'Then don't play around with what you don't know and don't understand!'

'I wasn't———'

'Oh, yes, you were! We've been together too long! Well, I'll tell you now, this is your final warning. It wouldn't take much to push me over the edge! So don't try it, unless you're sure you know what you're getting into!'

'I didn't know———' She stopped. She didn't know what? That his desire would be so raw and unforgiving, that his need would be so naked? But what had she expected? A man as masculine as Cal Fenton would hardly be otherwise.

His eyes stripped across her. 'Well, now you do! I can't think what I can do to spell it out plainer. I only hope you're a quick learner!' Abruptly he turned and vaulted up into the Land Rover, starting the engine before she had even collected her wits.

She got in leadenly and he let in the clutch. After a time he spoke, and his voice was cool and measured.

'If we keep heading west,' he said, 'we should

eventually hit the main loop-road through the park, then we can make our way back to the lodge.'

She looked at him closely with her green eyes. How could his mood change so fast?

When she did not reply Cal scowled across at her.

'If there's one thing I can't stand, it's people who sulk.'

'I'm not sulking, I'm thinking.'

'What about?'

'What do you think?'

He drove on for a few more minutes. Then he rapped out, 'OK. I apologise. I'd rather that hadn't happened—but in my book you asked for it.'

She turned his words over. It wasn't much of an apology, but she was surprised to get any at all.

'I'm sorry, too. I guess I was acting like a schoolgirl.'

His eyes went to hers, lingering across her face. His look was still hard. 'No,' he said roughly, 'not a schoolgirl. Unfortunately for me, definitely not a schoolgirl.' His eyes went back to the road, and his mouth crooked into a slight, self-deprecating grin. 'I somehow think we've lost that convent schoolgirl for good, somewhere along the way.'

Later, many weary hours later, they found the lodge, and Frankie lay in a deep bath, soaking away her tiredness and reviewing the headlong events of the past two days.

At least, she tried to, but her thoughts were like a rat on a wheel, and they turned endlessly and unerringly back to Cal.

She soaped a thigh. Cal's thighs were brown and muscled, she thought, and then swallowed at the memory of the way his hard body had assaulted hers, pushing her back against the Land Rover until she had longed to cry out in protest. Because that's what it had been, she knew—a deliberate, unrestrained assault, designed to frighten her off him.

She frowned. He wanted her, she knew that for certain. And over the past two days something else seemed to have grown up between them, a whole new web of respect and awareness.

Yet he seemed determined to keep her at arm's length, and she did not know why. He said it was her youth, her inexperience, but she sensed it was something else as well, something deeper, more primitive, that she could not begin to guess at. Or maybe it was something so simple that she could not bear to face it. Maybe there was a girlfriend waiting for him at home. After all, a man like Cal Fenton would hardly stay woman-less for long, and, although she had assumed his affairs were all fleeting, she actually knew nothing whatsoever about his private life.

She yawned, despite her churning thoughts, and soaped her other leg. Maybe tonight, over dinner, she could unravel the mystery. She would pin her hair up, wear the dress that had hitherto lain forgotten at the bottom of her basket, get him in the mood to talk. . . She blinked as her vision began to blur and, realising she was so weary that she was almost fainting, she got out of the water and stumbled towards the bed.

There she slept for hours, not waking until nine o'clock. Fumbling her way awake, she wondered why Cal had not called her for dinner. Then she saw the note pushed under the door. It was in the impatient black hand she was getting to know so well.

Frankie, I'm not going to let them get away with it. I'm still going to get those pictures. I've had to take the Land Rover, but I should be back in a couple of days. Charge everything to my account. Cal.

She read it twice, then sat slowly down on the bed. She felt bleak with disappointment, then a different feeling crept in. It was fear, deep fear for him and his safety. She remembered the shouting men with their menacing guns. If they caught Cal taking pictures of their activities they would hardly stop to think twice before they pulled their triggers. She shut her eyes, sick with dread, and the feeling closed like a blackness over her head.

This morning she had known she had fallen in love with Cal; now she knew it was something much worse. She wasn't just in love with him. Being in love was a passion that could blossom and fade—a mere question of flaring desire and short-term obsession. Just the sort of thing, in fact, that any observant outsider could have predicted for her, had he seen the two of them rattling off into the wilderness together. She grimaced at the thought, and at the innocent, unthinking girl she must have seemed then.

But what she felt for Cal was something altogether different. In him she had met her match, had found the one person who could make her whole; she did not know how she knew it, but she did, primitively and instinctively. And what she felt for him was love, real love, the kind that endured against all odds, and lasted for always. And the knowledge was like a huge, aching soreness in her heart.

Because Cal had no use for love, he had made that perfectly plain, and, even if it were otherwise, what could he possibly see in her? The answer was crystal clear, in his countless gibes about her youth and inexperience. 'Oh!' She groaned bitterly at the memory. Cal, she knew, felt a fleeting desire for her, but what was that compared to the burden of her love for him? He was her man, he would be for always, he held her in thrall. And the worst thing of all was that there was nothing she could do to change that fact— no matter how furiously he rejected her, it would stay that way forever.

CHAPTER NINE

Two days dragged past. Frankie's thoughts were always on Cal. After the peace and silence of the bush, the game lodge, with its milling crowds and souvenir kiosks, seemed like Piccadilly Circus, but she had to do something to pass the time so she joined the game-viewing buses that left the hotel every morning and evening.

Not that they ever saw much game, and any poor animal they came across was assailed by a battery of whirring video cameras. Animals watching animals, she thought, as people climbed and jostled across each other for the best view, and she turned her camera on her human companions rather than on the giraffes and gazelles that grazed near by.

It was hard to sleep. The nights were hot and her dreams were troubled. On the third night she tossed and turned for hours until she slipped into a restless doze in which she dreamt that Cal was in trouble, crying out, but when she fought to get to him, she could not get near.

'Oh!' She surfaced, crying and sweating, then sank back again, only to hear once more Cal's terrible cries.

She opened her eyes, registering her room, but the cries were still there, real shouts of pain and terror. She shot up, wide awake now, every nerve quivering like a cat sensing danger.

There was silence. Then it came again. Cal's voice, indistinct but terrible, coming from the next room.

Without thought, she shot out of bed and into his room. It was dark, and thick with sweat and fear. She stumbled over bags and clothes that had been discarded hastily. Some time in the night Cal must have returned and flung himself carelessly into bed.

Then the cry came again, its words urgent and indistinct. She heard muffled curses, then some clearer words. 'Leave me! I'm all right. Got to him——!' The tone of it made her blood run cold. She switched on the lamp. Cal lay naked in the bed, tangled in the sheet, his skin slicked with sweat. He was clearly ill. His face had a dreadful pallor, and his hand, extended, clutched convulsively.

'Oh!'

Frankie didn't know what to do. She looked around for a phone, but as she did so his body writhed and thrashed on the bed and his voice cried out, rising to the same pitch of agony. 'Damn you, I said leave me! Get to him—across the street—can't you see him?'

'It's all right!' She spoke instinctively, with no idea if he could hear her or not. 'They're seeing to him. Don't worry!'

He flung himself back towards her, catching at her wrist. His grip was like a vice. His eyes opened, but she could see at once that he was not seeing her, but looking straight through her to some terrible vision from the past. 'It just went up in his face. He took the full brunt——'

'Don't worry. Everything will be all right.'

'It should have been me—he pushed me back. It should have been me!'

She shushed him like a child, easing him back against the pillows, feeling terrified and alone. When his body untensed again, and he let her wrist go, she snatched up the phone. A sullen operator told her there was no chance of getting a doctor tonight. In the morning Cal could be evacuated by air ambulance if necessary, he said, but his tone made it clear he thought she was making an unnecessary fuss about a touch of flu.

'That might be too late! I have to do something now,' she shouted. 'At least get me someone I can talk to on the phone!' She slammed the receiver back down. Cal had flung himself face down again and was breathing with rapid, shallow breaths. She felt so helpless. She ran to the bathroom and fetched a cold flannel to sponge his face, but he was immediately covered in sweat again. His sheets were soaking.

He flung himself away from her, cursing furiously.

It was a fever. He must have caught a fever during his days out hunting the poachers. It was some ghastly tropical fever, and he was probably going to die of it! Panic gripped her as she bent to scrabble through his bag. After all, people did die, she knew it all too well. Her mother had gone out in the car and never come back. And her father had taken just one step too many towards an innocent-looking car that had blown up in his face.

Blown up in his face. She froze. What had Cal said? 'It went up in his face. He took the full brunt.' Her heart raced as his fevered words echoed through her head. 'It should have been me,' he'd said.

She shot round to look at him, as if by seeing his prone body she could read his mind. But the sight of him drove all thought from her head. He looked, if anything, worse. She had to do something, and fast. But what? She bent down again to his bag.

'Oh!' Tears were fogging her eyes, making her blind search useless. She dashed them away, her frightened moans joining Cal's fevered exclamations. What was the point of loving people when they just went and died on you? That must be how Cal felt—after all, he'd probably seen more people dead than alive.

She took a deep breath and struggled to get a grip on herself as she pulled out a wash-bag and began to rummage desperately through it, although what she was looking for she could not have said.

There were the usual sticking plasters and antiseptic creams and a few items she wished she hadn't seen, and then at the bottom a brown plastic pot of pills. She was just squinting at the label when the phone rang.

'Mrs Fenton?'

'Yes?' She answered without a moment's hesitation. The name was now as familiar as her own.

'My name is Dr Morton. I'm talking to you from Nairobi. I gather Mr Fenton is in a fever. Describe his symptoms to me.'

The calm, measured voice was immensely reassuring.

'Does your husband suffer from malaria, Mrs Fenton?' he asked, when she had finished.

'He's—er—he's never said. We haven't been married long,' she added lamely, 'but I found some pills in his bag.'

'Read the label to me.'

She read out the long, scientific words.

'Hmm, well, it's hard to be sure without being there, but I'm prepared to take a risk and say it seems like a straightforward case of malaria. Get him to take these according to the instructions and I'm sure he'll be back to normal fairly soon.'

'Oh, thank you!'

'You should see a steady recovery once he takes this medication. If his temperature is still as high in the morning, then we will have to think again, but I somehow don't think it will be.'

'Thank you. I'm sorry you had to be disturbed.'

'All part of the job. Goodnight, Mrs Fenton, and good luck.'

'Oh, Dr——'

'Yes?'

'Is there anything else I can do for him?'

'Sponge him down, keep him as comfortable as possible. That's the main thing. Get the hotel to send someone up to change his bed.'

'I'll do it myself,' she said quickly. She did not want strangers to see Cal in this distress. And when the doctor had gone she buzzed the desk clerk and demanded fresh sheets.

They arrived surprisingly promptly considering it was the middle of the night, along with a bowl she had also asked for. And when the wide-eyed maid had disappeared she set to work, systematically sponging him down. Either that, or the pills, seemed to calm him, because he lay still under her ministrations, even when she had to roll him this way, then that, to change his soaking sheets for fresh ones.

Finally she sponged his face with care, pushing his wet hair back from his skin and feeling the flannel rasp against the unshaven stubble of his beard. There were lines of tension on his forehead, and his jaw was gritted, but under her gentle ministrations his expression unclenched from whatever nightmare held him, and he seemed to sleep.

Exhausted, she lay beside him on the empty half of the double bed. His eyes were closed, the dark lashes fanned on cheeks that were still unnaturally pale, but his temperature seemed to have dropped a little. She grimaced with dry humour. She had dreamt of lying in bed with Cal, of exploring his naked body, and both things had come to pass. But hardly in a way either of them could have predicted.

Eventually his breathing became deeper and more natural. She swung her legs down and knelt before his open bag, planning to pack back the things she had thrown out in her earlier wild panic. At the bottom was a battered and dog-eared Filofax. She lifted it out, curious about all the clues it must hold to his life, and weighed it in her hand. She glanced over at the prone figure on the bed, sleeping quietly now, and back at the scuffed leather. Then, with masterly forbearance, she put it back in the bag. Next to it was a book. She lifted it out, wondering what Cal would choose for light reading. It was an unsurprising choice, a novel about India that had recently received rave reviews in all the book columns.

She flicked the pages and a sheaf of blue air-mail pages fell out. She marked the place from which they had fallen with her finger, and picked them up. Then curiosity got the better of her. Quiet as a burglar, she laid the book face down and smoothed the letter. Jealousy went through her like a knife as she read how it began.

My dearest Cal, How can we ever thank you enough for your continuing generosity to us all? We have nothing to give you except our love and our prayers, and the knowledge that without you the Kaloon Orphanage would never manage to stay in existence.

You will be pleased to hear that the hospital unit is finally finished and—blessings of blessings—Sister Frances has managed to find a qualified nurse who will come and give her services *free* for two days a week. She is also going to give the older children a health education lesson once a week. I'm sure if we had had that last year the cholera outbreak would not have been quite so devastating.

The other good news is that Jalan came back to us last week, after two months of living on the streets. I had feared he would be drawn into drug peddling, or worse—you know what life is like out there—but it seems not——

The letter ran on, full of warmth and life, and she read it absorbed, until it ended.

Please, my very dearest boy, look after yourself, and give yourself some mercy. I know that it is like whistling in the wind to ask you not to take so many risks, but I beg you to heed the wishes of an elderly woman who loves you dearly, and to try. Come and see us soon; it has been too long. Our love and prayers always.

Then there was an indistinguishable squiggle at the end.

Carefully Frankie folded it back into the book, and put the book and all the other things back into the bag.

Quietly she drew up a chair, and prepared to keep vigil by Cal's sleeping body. Then she looked deep into his face, withdrawn into a drugged sleep, and thought I don't know you at all.

CHAPTER TEN

CAL roused groggily once or twice the next day, took some water, and went back to sleep. The doctor telephoned and checked on his progress. Otherwise the day passed in silence, and it was not until the evening that his eyes snapped open and he was his old self again. He took in the sunset beyond the window at a glance.

'What happened to today?'

'The same thing as happened to last night—you were too feverish to notice.'

'What are you doing here?'

'Nursing you.'

'I don't need nursing!'

'No? You mean I should have left you alone and unconscious in a hotel room?'

'It's happened before.'

'I'm sure it has. Everything's happened to you before!'

His tone jarred on her already anxious nerves, making her snappish, but when she saw how he sank his head back to the pillows, obviously weary, she felt ashamed. 'You've had a malaria attack,' she said, more gently. 'You've been completely out of it for about sixteen hours.'

'Did you find the pills?'

'With a little help from the doctor.'

'A doctor? Oh, God! All I need is the pills.'

'Don't worry. He was only on the end of a telephone, he didn't set foot in here. Anyway, how was I to know it was malaria? For all I knew you could have been dying of green monkey fever. You looked ghastly, and you were shouting and screaming fit to bring the roof down.'

His eyes slid to hers. 'You really are your father's daughter, aren't you? Mike used to exaggerate, too.'

Her eyes narrowed. 'Mike? What made you think of him?'

He shrugged.

'Anyway, I'm not exaggerating. It woke me up, in the next room!' She stood up and went over to the bed. 'How do you feel, anyhow?'

'OK.'

'OK,' she echoed, cynically. Their glances snagged.

'Well, all right, I feel bloody wiped-out. I suppose you can see that. That's the way it takes you. But I'll be fine after I've rested up.'

'The doctor phoned back this morning. He said you ought to stay put for at least a couple of days.'

He uttered a short, sharp expletive. 'I don't need that sort of molly-coddling.'

'I just hope it was all worth it.'

'What do you mean?'

'The poachers; did you catch them in the act?'

'Oh!' He grinned at her, suddenly remembering, and his face warmed with a look that made her heart turn over so badly she had to look away. 'And how! I got some terrific stuff, and they didn't even know I was there.'

'Good.'

'I'm going to shave.' He eased himself up. 'If you're a lady, you'll avert your gaze.'

'You forget I've given you several blanket-baths in the night.'

'Ah, so you've plumbed the mysteries of my body, have you, Frankie?' He forced a grin, but his eyes on hers were watchful and his voice wary. 'How about the secrets of my mind?'

'I don't know what you're talking about.'

'All that shouting and screaming you say I did—did it add up to anything coherent?'

She held his eyes. All kinds of questions jostled to be voiced, but she saw something in his look, a guardedness, that made her lie smoothly, 'No, not really. It was all very muffled.'

He got out of bed and she looked away.

'If we aren't going to stay here, what are we going to do?'

'Go to the coast.'

The bathroom door closed behind him. When he came out again, a towel round his hips, he got back into bed without a word. He was white, and she could see that the effort of shaving had exhausted him.

'Great!' she said. 'I've been looking forward to seeing the sea. How long will it take us from here?'

'*Me*. Take *me*. This is a vacation I plan to take alone.'

'But you can't! You can't drive!'

'I just did.' He flexed his shoulder, then grimaced. 'I'll get by.'

'But——!'

'But what?'

She struggled to make her voice light. 'I've been up

all night giving bed-baths and changing sheets; I think I deserve a trip to the beach!'

'No one asked you to turn nurse.'

'Oh!' She scowled in exasperation. 'Some men might say thank you!'

'I'm not "some men".'

'So you're sacking me? Just like that?'

'You can drive me to Nairobi, and I'll sort out your ticket home. You'll get your full wages.'

'I don't care about the money!' She turned away so that he would not see the tears of frustrated disappointment that sprang to her eyes.

'Well, I'm afraid that's all that's on offer.' Cal contemplated the gathering dark outside the window. 'Do you know what it's like down there? All powder-white sands and waving palms? It's the most sensuous place on earth. If we go there together——' He shrugged.

Suddenly she turned, and her voice tore across him. 'So what? So what if we go there together? So what if we have an affair? If I don't care, why should you?' she shouted. 'You know what I think? I think all this nobility of yours, this restraint, is nothing at all to do with my age, or my innocence. It's because of who I am! If it was any other twenty-year-old you wouldn't think twice. But I'm Mike O'Shea's daughter! And that, for some reason, puts me beyond the pale! Oh——' Abruptly she began to choke on her words, tiredness and frustration raging within her.

Cal closed his eyes, and his voice when it came was like cracking ice. 'The only thing I think is that I'd like some sleep. Alone. In private. So will you please just get the hell out of here and don't come back until you're invited? And that's an order!'

Without a word, she jumped up and ran to the door, tears fogging her eyes so blindly that she had to fumble for the handle before she could slam her way out. Then she threw herself across her own bed and sobbed bitterly until she had no more tears to shed and an exhausted sleep finally overcame her.

It was not until midday the next day that he rapped sternly on her door. 'Come on, we're leaving.'

'I'll be glad to!'

She marched ahead of him, down the stairs, in silence, and stood seething while he paid the bill.

'I trust you've eaten,' he observed coolly, 'because it's a long haul back to town.'

She flashed him a glance. He looked pale and haggard.

'What is it to you if I haven't?'

'I hope to God we're not going to have this bad temper all the way to Nairobi. The way I feel, I could well do without it.'

'Then you should have stayed and got some rest, just like the doctor ordered! But you wouldn't, would you? You're too damn stubborn!'

'I don't need lectures from you on what I should and shouldn't be doing! I've managed perfectly well without them so far, and I intend to keep it that way!'

They faced each other, eyes blazing with antagonism.

'Just like you don't need nursing, I suppose! Or anyone to do your driving any more. Well, that's fine by me! Absolutely fine!'

Blind with anger she marched out to the Land Rover,

threw her basket carelessly into the back, and swung up into the passenger-seat.

'What the hell do you think you're doing?'

'I'm going to Nairobi to be put on a plane!'

'But *you're* driving to the city!'

'Am I? Who says? I thought I'd been dismissed.'

'I still want you to drive me today.'

He scowled with fury. She smiled sweetly across into his dark gaze. 'That's what you want, is it? Well, what about what I want? Maybe I'd just like to look at the scenery for a change.'

'Why you——!'

Frankie looked pointedly away from him and put her sunglasses on.

'It's the best part of a day's drive——'

'But you're quite capable of driving again now. You told me so last night.' She glanced at him again and saw dark circles under his eyes, and beads of sweat on his brow, and she almost relented. But as she wavered he rose to her challenge, his jaw set grimly.

'All right, then——' He got in and started the engine, scouring her with a dark look. 'I know perfectly well what your game is, and it won't work. Not for a minute.'

'I don't have a game.'

'Yes, you do. You're trying to prove a point. Trying to force me to take you to the beach with me.'

'No, I'm not. I don't want to go anywhere with you any more!' she burst out, and was surprised to realise it was true. She had come to the end of her tether, had had as much as she could take of his cold rejection. 'I'm just thoroughly sick and tired of everything! But if this is to be my last day in Africa, then I want to take in all I can.'

For a moment Cal scrutinised her closely, trying to assess the truth of her words, then he let in the clutch, and they set off.

Three hours later he pulled over on the pitted, sandy track, and stopped. Wearily he climbed down and leaned against the vehicle. She got out too, and walked round to him.

'Are we admiring the view?'

'Stop it, Frankie, I've had enough. In every way.' His voice was so hard that it grated down her spine, and when she looked at his face she knew why. He was in a feverish sweat again, and one hand held his sore shoulder. He had driven until he was ready to collapse, and she had sat there and let him. She had intended to teach him a lesson, to show him how much he needed her, but she had never meant it to go this far.

'Oh!' She pressed her hands to her mouth, horrified and ashamed at the sight of him. Her heart contracted for his pain and weariness.

'You win,' he said. 'I might just about have made it from Nairobi to the coast, but I can't make it all the way.'

'I wasn't trying to win anything!'

'Well, whatever.'

'You might not have made it to the coast. You might have ended up in this state halfway there—on your own.'

'Maybe. Maybe not. Whatever the case, you'd better take over.'

'To where? Nairobi, or the coast?'

He shrugged wearily. 'Oh, what the hell? To the

coast, I suppose.' And then he sank into the passenger-seat and appeared to sleep throughout the long, hot journey to Mombasa.

When, at long last, they neared the coast, she touched his arm. His eyes flickered open, grey, familiar depths resting on hers, making her swallow. She pulled her fingers away from his bare flesh. 'I need directions.'

He levered himself up and looked around. 'You came all this way without stopping?'

'We did stop, twice, for petrol, but you were asleep.'

He dashed a hand through his hair. 'We don't want to go right into the town centre. If you turn down here you can skirt the worst of the traffic. The house is out on the beach, to the north.'

They turned down increasingly bumpy side-roads until they were following a dusty yellow track through what looked like fields of sugar cane. She was fascinated by the change in the scenery. They had left behind the high grassy plains long ago, were now in steamy, tropical surroundings.

'Here.'

She turned through a gap in the hedge, and pulled up by a modest wooden house.

'Oh! It really is on the beach! Right on it.' Frankie jumped down and at once the heat enfolded her like a blanket, making her shorts and T-shirt feel thick and heavy. Ahead of the house was a short stretch of palm-studded garden, and immediately beyond that lay a glittering white beach, and the sea.

Cal got down more slowly, but he seemed happy to be here. His whole demeanour seemed to relax and grow more easy. He led the way into the house. She followed him.

'Oh!' She looked round doubtfully.

'What's the matter?'

'I can see why you wanted to be alone here—it's lovely, but it's very small.'

'It's no problem. I'll drag a pallet on to the veranda. I usually do anyway. You can have the bedroom.'

'Even so——' She could not have put it into words, but she knew immediately that this was Cal's real home, his private bolt-hole from the world. She turned around, looking at everything. The little house was simply furnished, but in the dim light that filtered through the closed slatted shutters she could see that it glowed with the rich colours of African fabrics and Indian rugs. She caught sight of interesting-looking carvings, of etchings and photographs on the walls, a calabash standing by the door. There were books and magazines and a stack of music tapes. It was everything that his stiff and formal house wasn't, she thought, and she knew she was an interloper.

'How do you feel now?' she asked him.

'Much better. That sleep on the way down did me the world of good.'

'Good.' It was good news, but she felt despondent. Now he needed her no longer, and would soon start to push her away again.

'Why don't you make a cup of tea, and I'll get the bags in?'

'No.'

'We've got no milk?'

'No, I mean yes. Yes, we've got no milk. But that's not it.' She summoned all her resources. 'I'm not staying. I just wanted to make sure you got here safely. I'm going straight back to Nairobi.' Over his shoulder, through the open door, the sand and the sea and the palm trees beckoned. She cast them a brief, longing glance, then looked back to him. She stuffed her hands resolutely into her shorts pockets. In the dim light he was a dark outline, mysterious and compelling.

'You don't have to.'

'I want to!'

He strode across the room and began throwing open the shutters, so that the late afternoon sun flooded in, lighting her expression.

'For one thing, how do you plan to get back?'

'It depends if you want to hang on to the Land Rover or not. If you don't, I'll drive. If you do, I can get a shared taxi. I read about them in a guide-book.'

'I do. And anyway, it's dangerous for a woman to travel by herself at night.' His face was grim. She could see he meant it.

'Oh.'

'Leave it for now. We can sort things out in the morning.'

'I'm just so tired of being in your way,' she burst out, 'and of you telling me I am! I want to get out!'

Something in her tone made him come swiftly over to her, and take her shoulders.

'Frankie, you're not in my way, believe me. I know that after the things I've said you probably won't, but it's the truth.' His eyes searched her face and what he saw there made him frown. 'Apart from anything else, you're exhausted from all that driving. You need to rest as much as I do.'

'But I know you want to be here alone!'

'Did. Now I'm not so sure.' His mouth crooked a little, inviting her to smile. 'We've been together so long, I'm beginning to wonder if I can manage without our daily argument.'

'Well I can!' she cried bitterly. 'Easily.'

'All right, then. Let's agree we'll have no arguments. And no more talk about going back to Nairobi tonight. OK? Just take my word for it that you are a very welcome guest, and let's settle in.'

He stayed holding her firmly until she slowly nodded, then he dropped his hands and began to drag a mattress on to the veranda. Quietly she fetched her basket of clothes and his bag, and put them by their separate beds. Cal was somewhere in the back of the house, starting up the hot-water system. She slipped off her shoes and padded around on bare feet, finding the bathroom and the kitchen. The house smelled of heated wood, and the boards of the shaded veranda were warm under her feet.

Cal came back. He had stripped off his T-shirt and wore only shorts. She fought not to look at his body. The body she knew so well, she thought, every intimate detail. He was whistling, something she'd never heard him do before. 'Do you like it?'

'It's lovely!'

He nodded towards the beach. 'There's nothing like a swim to freshen up after a long journey.'

She looked longingly at the blue water. 'I've got no bathing costume.'

'It doesn't matter. I could guarantee you'd be alone. No one comes down here.'

'What about you?'

'I won't look.'

'I didn't mean that. I meant are you going to swim?'

He shook his head. 'I'm convalescent, remember?

Starting that generator wore me out for the rest of the day.'

Her eyes opened in surprise at his new willingness to be frank about his condition, but he affected not to notice. 'Off you go.'

'I ought to make that tea.'

'No, I've just noticed, it's nearly sundowner time. When you come back I'll fix us both something long and strong.'

'Do you think that's wise?'

'You mean in my condition?'

'No, I mean in our condition,' she said bluntly. 'Remember what you said about the waving palms?'

He gave her a long, bewitching smile. 'Malaria shuts down all your systems pretty effectively, Frankie. This is probably the one night of the year when I can guarantee your virtue with impunity.'

It was more than an hour later when she walked back towards the house through the palm trees, languorous from the tropical sea. She paused as Cal came into view. He was sitting on his mattress on the veranda, a straw hat tipped over his eyes, his back against the wall, and his legs sprawled before him. At first she thought he was asleep. Then she realised he was methodically dusting and cleaning his camera lens, and listening to a tape on a personal stereo as he did so.

He was so utterly absorbed that she allowed herself the luxury of feasting her eyes on him. She saw his strong shoulders and the bronzed flatness of his stomach, the play of his sure hands and the muscled length of his legs.

When she had tended him in his illness, sponging

away the sweat of his fever, she had disciplined herself to have a medical detachment to the lines and planes beneath her hands. Now, though, her memories rose up and her blood beat at the knowledge of the sculpted lines of his body, the way the chest narrowed to slim hips and firm buttocks and a powerful manhood. She had no first-hand comparisons, but she knew enough to know that he was beautiful, and that she ached for him in every atom of her being.

'Oh!' She groaned softly and her hand tightened, longing to know the feeling of his body beneath her palm, but all she felt was the coarse roughness of palm tree bark beneath her fingers.

She walked back to the house. Cal looked up as her shadow fell across him. She waved to him, lost as he was in his private, musical world, and mouthed that she was going to have a shower. She felt hot and sweaty, and wished she had something floating and cool to wear instead of her shorts.

She padded into her room. By the bed was a carved sea trunk, and she opened it. Inside were spare sheets, cushions, and some beautiful lengths of printed cottons. She knew what they were. She had seen African women wearing them as sarongs, twisted above their breasts, of using them as slings to carry their treacle-eyed babies on their backs. She selected one in the colours of the sea and the sand, and twisted it around her slight figure. Then she fluffed out her hair to dry, and went to find Cal.

He looked up and pulled down his earphones. 'You've gone native.'

'Do you mind? I found it in the trunk.'

His eyes went all over her figure, very dark. For a

moment she thought she must have done the wrong thing.

'I'll take it off if you want; I shouldn't have plundered your things——'

But he shook his head. 'Don't. You look stunning. It's just that it belonged to an old girlfriend of mine. It gave me a strange turn seeing you like that.'

An old girlfriend. So this was not such a bolt-hole after all. 'I'll take it off.'

'No, don't. She was someone I was with years ago. And she never meant much to me anyway.'

'Does anyone?' The blurted words fell rudely in the space between them before she could bite them back. He squinted up at her, under his hat. She held her breath, steeling herself for his anger. But he only said, 'You tell me. You spoke like someone who knows the answer.'

Her chin lifted at the challenge. 'I don't know. You certainly seem perfectly self-contained and——' she faltered '—and after what you've seen, you're probably. . .' Her words tailed away.

'Hardened? Cynical?'

'Yes. I suppose so. Anyway, that's what you as good as told me the other night.'

He laid his camera lens back in its case. She watched the movement of his hands.

'If it's true, it's hardly surprising. After all, I can either look at you standing there now and see a lovely young girl, perfect in every detail, or I can see the blood and guts you would make if you happened to be blown up by a land-mine, or the haggard, haunting figure you would turn into if you happened not to eat for a month or so——'

'My father saw all those things too, but he didn't cut himself off from life. Just the opposite. He knew how fragile and temporary everything was, so he wanted to reach out and grasp every moment with both hands.'

'I'm not your father!' Cal looked sharply up at her, then down. 'Although I often wish I had been!'

'What?' She blinked, unsure that she had heard the words she thought she had heard. 'What do you mean?'

There was a long silence, and then, smiling a strained smile, he began to lever himself up. 'This is much too heavy a conversation for my fragile condition. I'll make us some drinks. Why don't you listen to that?' He nodded at the stereo. 'I always find Mozart very restorative.'

He came back with a clinking pitcher. 'Vodka and tonic, with lots of fresh lime. I reckoned the quinine would be good for me.'

'Quinine?'

'In the tonic. It isn't just chance that the old colonials were so partial to gin and tonic, you know.'

'No, I didn't.' She sipped her drink. It was icy fresh and delicious. She drank more, wanting to blot out the puzzle of his muttered words, because she knew he would not explain them.' I ought to think about supper. I see there's a box of food in the kitchen.'

'My housekeeper left it. I ordered it before I went down with malaria. And you don't have to think about anything. Stop behaving like a fussy housewife and enjoy your drink and the sunset.'

He sank down next to her on the mattress. She could feel the heat of his skin. She drank deeply, and the cold liquid made a little explosion of fire in her empty stomach, making her feel free and careless. 'I can't win with you. One moment I'm an innocent little virgin, the next a fussy housewife.'

He took a draught from his drink, then held the glass loose in a dangling hand. 'You realise, of course, that the former probably wouldn't apply any more if we'd had to huddle together in that poachers' tent for more than one night,' he said, matter-of-factly. 'We'd have had to have found some way to keep warm.'

Frankie remembered distinctly the feeling of his body, hardened against her.

She giggled. 'You realise, of course, that I wouldn't have exactly minded——'

'It wasn't a good idea.' He slanted her a glance. 'It isn't now. It never will be.'

'So you've said. I'm losing track of the number of times.'

'For heaven's sake, Frankie, be sensible. You could end up pregnant, for one thing!'

'That's just an excuse—and a dishonest one!'

'What do you mean?'

'I had to look through your things when you were ill, to find your pills.' She blushed, but held his gaze.

It took a second or two for her meaning to sink in. Then he threw back his head and roared with laughter. 'I first packed my travelling-kit more than a decade ago, when I was a very impetuous young man! I'm ashamed to say that it hasn't been properly unpacked since. I'm sure the "things" to which you so delicately refer passed their expiry date years ago. I certainly wouldn't ever choose to put them to the test.'

Frankie eyed him doubtfully, and he mocked her with a raised eyebrow. 'Don't tell anyone, though, will you? It would absolutely ruin my image!'

'I think your image is robust enough to stand a few knocks.' She looked wistfully out to sea. 'You've filled hundreds of inches in the gossip columns in your time. It's ironic, really, when you think about it—us being here like this, and you such a known womaniser.'

'Taking women out doesn't always mean taking them home, at least, not in my book.' He looked at her. 'When I come home from an assignment I find it's better to keep busy. If I sit at home thinking——' He shrugged. 'That way madness lies.'

'So you go out and about on the town. And you're never short of a beautiful woman to hang on your arm.'

'Breadth if not depth,' he said lightly.

She sighed. 'It's not surprising, really, with your looks, and your name.'

'I don't know about that. What I have discovered is that there are some women who seem to love the scent of danger. War groupies——' his voice twisted '—who hang around as if they're hoping to smell cordite on my clothes!'

'They've only seen the films.' She thought about Mike. 'They don't know what it really means.'

He took in her words in silence for a moment, then he said, 'Tell me what else you found in my luggage?'

'A letter,' she confessed. 'It fell out of a book. I didn't mean to read it, but then I did.'

'And?'

'And it made me wonder if you're quite as hard-bitten as you like to pretend.'

He swallowed deeply on his drink, and scanned the sea for a long time before he answered. 'If you're looking for a heart of gold, forget it.'

'A redeeming feature or two would be quite enough.'

Cal looked at her sharply. 'You mean, you really think I'm that bad?' He drank again, and when he spoke his tone was lighter. 'Then you must only want me for my body.'

She grinned, despite herself. 'Your body is very nice—as I discovered when I had to play nurse the other night. As to whether you're that bad, I don't know the answer. All I know is that the letter was a surprise to me.'

He was silent for a time. Then he said, 'I make a lot of money out of what I do, money that I don't have much use for. I give some to an orphanage in India, that's all.'

'Some? Or a lot?'

'It's all relative. What is some to me, is a lot to them. Anyway, I like the kids. Some of them come from the most appalling backgrounds, yet they seem to bob up smiling. And the nuns are saints. There's no other word for them.'

'So human nature isn't all bad?'

'I never said it was. I've just seen rather too much of the negative side——'

'For your own good,' she finished, unaware that she was speaking.

He smiled. 'If you say so, Nurse.'

She smiled back at him. 'I'm sorry I read it, though. I shouldn't have.'

'Forget it. I would have done the same.' For a time they were silent, both staring out towards the dark sea. Then she said, 'That was the orphanage in the film, wasn't it? The television film about you. It showed you with the children. I remember how you crouched down in the dust and showed them your camera. Your face looked different when you talked to them.'

'You saw it, that ghastly film? I tried to stop them making it, but they were determined. It made me look a hero, but I'm not. I'm just someone who happens to be there when things happen.'

'What sort of things?' Her voice grew sharper, remembering his muffled outbursts in the night.

'All kinds of things, things you couldn't dream of. Most of them I try to forget, once I've finished the job in hand.'

'But you don't forget, do you? You have troubled dreams.'

'Do I? You seem to know a lot about it.'

'When you were feverish——'

'When *anyone* is feverish, they have lurid dreams,' he cut in swiftly. 'It's all to do with the body temperature.'

'Yours must be worse than most. Do you remember them afterwards?' She held her breath, wondering what he would say if he did, whether he would explain his terrible cries. But he only looked deep into the bottom of his glass and, after a long moment, he said smoothly, 'No, not a thing. Not a single thing.'

CHAPTER ELEVEN

THAT night Frankie slept for hours and hours, and woke the next day to the faint wash of the sea and a springing sense of well-being.

At once she wrapped her sarong around her, and stepped out into the glittering morning. Cal lay asleep on the veranda, a sheet over his hips, and the brown length of his back bare. One arm was flung above his head and his hand lay open, the fingers uncurled and trusting. It seemed that his dreams had been peaceful, and she was glad for him.

The sea was as warm as a bath. She swam for a long time, relishing the idyllic scene. Then she rewound her sarong, and began to walk back to the house.

Cal was coming down to the beach, a towel round his hips. Last night's sleep had driven the last traces of pallor from his face, and he seemed completely restored to health.

'Are you going in? It's lovely.'

'Mmm.'

His eyes flickered over her damp hair and thin cotton clothing. Immediately her body began to beat for him, and she knew with a sinking heart that, with him restored to full health, sexual tension would rise up and snap at their heels like a vicious dog once more. Last night's companionable truce was already a thing of the past.

Their eyes met and sparked with the knowledge that they both shared.

'I'll make us some breakfast,' she said, and went quickly on, but she could not resist stopping and watching his distant figure as he threw off his towel and sauntered naked into the sea.

She had to leave. She knew she had to. Everything here, from the luscious papaws she was slicing for breakfast to the enchanting whisper of the tropical ocean, was a feast for the senses. It heated her blood and stirred her pulses until she ached for Cal with a need that was close to despair. There was no way she could stay with him here, alone, if he did not take her into his arms. And yet he wouldn't. She knew he wouldn't. A cessation of hostilities was the most he would give her.

She vowed to tell him at the first good opportunity, yet all morning he sat absorbed on the veranda, painstakingly restoring his camera equipment to order. She discovered a shelf full of books on photography, and retreated with them to a distant part of the garden where, behind the screen of a large flowering bush, she loosened her sarong to her waist and let the sun colour her skin.

Hours passed in a hum of crickets and a gentle wash of waves.

'Are you learning anything?'

Cal came strolling barefoot round the bush. She sat up suddenly.

He regarded her small breasts with their delicate nipples quite openly, and they tightened and peaked instantly in response to his look. His eyes went to hers as he saw the effect he had on her. 'I don't want to be personal, but the sun's very hot now. I wouldn't want you to get sunburned in sensitive places.'

'I *was* lying on my stomach—until you came along.'

'I would have knocked, but I couldn't find the door.'

She stood up, and pulled up her sarong. He watched her frankly as she tied it. 'It seems a pity,' he observed, crooking his mouth. 'Going topless is a way of life in Africa. But under the circumstances——'

'Quite.'

Damn him! she thought savagely, marching ahead of him back to the house. How could he stay so cool and collected when he knew exactly what he did to her with just one glance? Why wasn't he tempted just to take her in his arms? Or did he get some sort of perverse kick from this painful sexual teasing?

He followed her. She whirled round.

'I want to go back to Nairobi, Cal. As soon as possible! Preferably now!'

She banged into her bedroom, and came out again dressed in her shorts and T-shirt.

'What a very tempestuous girl you are,' he said. 'If it's not one thing it's another. Anyway, "now" is a bit hard to arrange.' She glared at him, her eyes a green fire of anger.

'Look, if it's because of what I just said, I was only teasing.' His eyes went over her face. 'I'm trying to keep the atmosphere light.'

'The atmosphere isn't light! It hasn't been for days! It probably never will be! And you know it. You might be able to keep up the pretence, but I can't!'

His expression tightened, all warmth fading from his look. 'Of course I know it! Why do you think I was so keen to come here alone in the first place? But since I couldn't make it, and since I'm painfully aware of how much I owe you for what you've done for me over the past couple of days, I'm trying my damndest to keep things pleasant! However, since it obviously isn't enough, then you're right. You'd better go.'

'You don't owe me a thing. I did what I would have done for anyone, even a sick dog!'

'Charming!' He dashed a hand through his hair, scowling at her.

'Just find me a telephone, and I'll fix up a flight.'

'There's no need for that; I was going into Mombasa anyway this afternoon. You can come with me.' He walked away across the veranda to stare out at the sea. 'It's probably of no interest to you at all, since you clearly want as little as possible to do with me, but I've been thinking about your pictures. I have a friend in Mombasa who's a photographer. He's got his own darkroom. I planned to run off some of my poaching films, and I thought you might like me to print up some of your stuff, to see what you've come up with.'

'Oh!' Frankie felt caught off-balance, entirely wrong-footed. 'I'd love it—but shouldn't you be resting?'

'I'm fine now, as long as I take it slowly for a few days. But too much inactivity isn't good for me, especially here and now.' He shot her a glance. 'Despite what you think, pretending is very hard work. My thoughts keep straying off in unwelcome directions.'

'Then you'll be glad I'm going. It'll make life a lot easier—for both of us!'

There was a pause. Then he said coldly, 'I dare say it will. It certainly couldn't be any more difficult.'

He dropped her in the centre of town and told her to meet him in two hours.

'Where can I find a travel agent?'

'Wait till I've finished. Then I'll sort things out for you. I know the best people.'

She shot him a doubtful look, but he only glanced at her harshly.

'Don't worry, I mean it. I want an end to all this every bit as much as you do—if not more!'

Frankie slammed the door of the Land Rover, and wandered around Mombasa in a daze. Under any other circumstances she would have loved walking the streets of the heat-soaked town, watching the Arab dhows, with their carved prows, ride at anchor, and seeing the baskets of ripe mangoes offered for sale on the pavements. But she felt exhausted and irritated, and the sailors who jostled along the narrow streets and wolf-whistled at her slender, tanned figure only heightened her mood.

She was glad when it was five o'clock and she could make her way to the wide terraced bar of the St George's Hotel and wait for Cal.

She looked around. On all sides other women sat alone at tables, toying with their drinks, but it was clear that in this bustling port they were waiting not for friends, but for customers. She was grinning grimly to herself, thinking how shocked her aunt would be to see her in such company, when a youth with a pronounced Liverpool accent began to pull back a chair next to hers.

'Mind if I join you?'

'Actually I'm waiting for someone.'

He didn't seem to hear. 'My name's Shane. We're

on manoeuvres here. What do you think of Mombasa, then?'

She guessed from his shiny, wet eyes that he'd spent his shore-leave drinking his way through the town.

'I think it's lovely. I'd think it was even better if I could enjoy my drink in peace.'

''S nice meeting an English girl. The other ones. . .' He nodded his head around the bar. 'You can't talk to them properly. They only want your wallet.'

'How interesting.' She made her voice as brittle as ice. It was lost on her drunken companion. He grinned wolfishly at her. 'What's your name, then?'

'Jane, Shane,' she said coldly, and swivelled away from him, longing for Cal to come.

Cal.

For a moment or two she had forgotten him, but her heart leapt up knowing she would see him again soon. Even two hours away from him seemed like a lifetime. What on earth would a real lifetime be like? How would she ever bear it? But Shane had finally got the message, and didn't like it one bit.

'Here, you toffee-nosed bitch!' His hand grabbed her arm, dragging her round to face him. As she did, she caught sight of Cal from the corner of her eye. He was standing darkly on the terrace steps, a packet of photographs under his arm, his face set, his eyes glittering with a depth of anger she had never seen before. She took him in like the frozen frame from a film, and the image of his palpable fury made her mouth go dry. Surely he didn't think she was encouraging this lout!

'No one turns their back on Shane Hutton.'

'On the contrary, buster, it's probably the most sensible thing anyone can do!'

Before she realised what was happening, Cal's hand was on the back of Shane's neck, lifting him like a toy and hustling him to the steps. 'Off you go, back to playing sailors,' he said, and threw him roughly on his way. Cheers and laughter erupted from the other drinkers, but he ignored them, grabbing her wrist as roughly as he had handled Shane Hutton.

'Come on. Out.'

'What the hell are you doing? Let me go!'

He pulled her through the maze of tables, thrust her into the Land Rover, jumped in, and revved the engine.

'How dare you——?'

He ignored her, threading through the afternoon rush-hour as if demons were after them.

'What about getting my ticket?'

'To hell with your ticket!'

She shot him a furious glance, but it was no competition for the raging fury on his face.

'You surely didn't think I was encouraging him?'

'I don't know what I think! What I do know is that the town's ten times rougher than it used to be. It's no place for a girl to be on her own.'

'You're crazy! I was perfectly all right.'

He did seem crazy. He was driving at the limits of safety, cursing at the traffic that slowed their pace. He snapped her a brief, grey look. 'Who knows? Maybe I am!' he bit out, then looked back at the busy road. 'But I hardly think now is the right moment to discuss something as serious as my sanity!'

'Oh!' She slumped back in exasperation, rubbing her

wrist where he had hurt her, and watched the scenery speed by until they were free of the town again and turning into the drive of the beach-house.

She got down, walked round to the veranda, and slumped on to the warm wooden steps without a word. Anger and confusion raged like a tide within her. She heard Cal go into the house and throw his photographs carelessly on a table. Then he was behind her, propping himself up in the doorway, his arms folded across his chest. She couldn't see him, but she could feel him, his vibrations as strong as a touch against her skin.

'Aren't you going to ask me about your pictures?' he said, in an infuriatingly normal voice. 'You can see them if you want.'

'No.'

'Well, I'll tell you anyway. They were sensational. Absolutely amazing for an amateur. You've got a natural eye.'

She hugged her knees, not saying anything.

'John, my friend, said the same.'

Still she could not speak. Her anger with him swamped out all other feelings.

'The ones you took of the tourists in the game park were the most original. They gave a whole new angle to the usual African wildlife pictures. Shall I tell you what I did?'

He waited, then, when he saw that she was still not going to speak, he said, 'I printed up the best and sent them off to Doug MacArthur, the pictures editor of the *Sunday Globe*, to see what he thinks. I'm sure he'll want to run them.'

'Did you?'

'Well, I can see you're so thrilled you can hardly contain yourself.'

Frankie looked ahead of her. The tropical darkness was falling heavily, and to her heightened nerves the whirr of the cicadas and the thick warmth seemed as full of portent as a gathering storm. Then she looked back. He was a dark shadow in the doorway.

'What do you want me to do? Bow down and kiss your feet with gratitude?'

'A bit of simple enthusiasm might be nice. I was so excited when I saw what you'd come up with, I wanted to find you and drag you over there to see for yourself.'

'But instead you dragged me off that hotel terrace, in front of all those people, like some wild Tarzan act——' She rubbed at her wrist. 'I don't know what got into you.' There was a silence. 'And I don't suppose you'll explain either, because you never do,' she burst out bitterly. 'You just go your own way, do exactly what you want to do, and to hell what anyone else thinks or feels. Well, I'm sick of it, absolutely sick of it! I've had enough. I want to get out. I wanted to get out this afternoon, but no, suddenly I'm driven back here on some peculiar whim of yours! I tell you, if you go on like this——'

'Yes, Frankie?' Cal's voice twisted coldly. 'Do go on.'

She shook her head blindly.

'You want to save me from myself?'

The acid tone touched such a raw spot in her jangling nerves that she was suddenly on her feet and shouting like a mad woman. 'No! No, I don't. I wouldn't bother. I think you enjoy it too much—being the dark stranger, the hardened loner, the man who's seen it all. But you know what?'

'No, no, I don't. Why don't you tell me?' His voice had grown still colder, full of ice and steel, as hers heated with rage. There was something in it, a razor's edge of danger, that told her she should stop, but she didn't, she couldn't.

'I think you've seen everything and nothing! You think you know so much about life, yet you know nothing! You don't let anything touch you! You don't feel anything! You don't love anything!'

With one stride he was in front of her, his face glowing with anger. 'Is that what you think? Well, that's very interesting! Now shall I tell you what I think? What I think is that I've had about as much as I can take from you, Frankie O'Shea! I'm sick of your home-spun philosophies, your endless moralising, the way you're always so certain you know best. I might not know much about life, but you know nothing at all! For a start, you've no idea what it's taken for me to keep my hands off you these last few weeks! Now I'm beginning to wonder why I bothered——'

'Nobody asked you to!'

'Haven't you ever done anything unasked?'

'Oh, you like to pretend you're so noble and good, but it's really only self-preservation. You'll take any amount of physical risks—wars and floods and fires don't scare you one bit—but you're absolutely petrified of any emotional risk!'

'You presume to know me so well!' His voice ripped over her.

'I do!' Her eyes blazed at his. 'Don't ask me how, or why, I just know I do. Just as you know me. We always have, right from the beginning! Right from that very first day! We might not like what we know, but we know it just the same!'

They were standing close together, breathing hard like runners in a race. She saw his face, harsh and unforgiving. Then his hands were gripping her shoulders as his eyes stripped over her open, angry face. 'The only thing I know about you,' he whispered intently, 'is that you're driving me half out of my senses! One minute all I want to do is to slap some sense into you. The next, I see your hair, your eyes, that devastating smile, and I can't think of anything beyond how much I want to hold you and kiss you and make love to you until I can't think straight any more!' He shook her in frustration, pushing her back against the post of the veranda. 'Why the hell did it have to be like this?'

'I don't know. I didn't want it any more than you did! I only wanted to go to Africa! I didn't mean to be such a millstone round your neck!'

'A millstone. Oh, God, is that what you think?'

'It's not what I think. It's what you told me.'

'Then I didn't know what I was saying!' His eyes tore over her lips, her breasts, her bare brown arms. 'Or maybe I did. Maybe I knew exactly what I was saying, if a millstone is something they tie you to, to drown you.' His lips parted as he looked at hers, and she saw the dangerous whiteness of his teeth. 'I've been drowning in you ever since I met you,' he got out, and as he did she saw something deep within him shift and change, as if a floodgate had opened, and his passion, so long held back, finally swamped all restraint. 'Or at least my reason has,' he groaned, and then his lips

were coming down on hers, hard and seeking, taking
her as if he could not get enough of her sweetness.

'Oh!' She moaned at the feelings he touched instantly
in her, and staggered against him as her legs started to
shake.

He shifted to hold her more firmly, then kissed her
harder, opening her mouth and taking its softness with
his tongue. It was like no kiss she had ever known, but
deeper and more urgently full of possibilities and desire
than she could have dreamt of.

He broke from her, his chest heaving slightly, but his
lips still found her throat and neck.

'Oh, the smell of you, the touch. . .' His hands
roamed her shoulders. 'You're so soft, so beautiful.
I've lain awake at night, aching for you.'

'And I for you! More than you can imagine.'

Restlessly his lips touched her hair, and she reached
her hands up to his shoulders and drew his mouth back
to hers.

She felt no shame, no false modesty as she let him
see how much she longed to mould her body to his.
His hands stroked her shoulders and arms, then over
all the curves of her body. Impatiently he began to
shrug off her T-shirt and shorts, and she moved to help
his expert fingers.

'Let me look at you,' he commanded, and held her
away from him. She felt his eyes lingering over the
swells and curves of her figure, and was proud in the
knowledge that he was the first man to see her like
this.

'God forgive me,' he murmured, pulling her close to
him, 'but I've undressed you so often in my mind——'
He bent his head and kissed the curves of her breasts,

taking each in turn with his mouth. She caressed the thickness of his hair as his head bent to her, and felt desire arrow through her so sharply that she could hardly bear it.

'Please——' she heard herself say, and then she was tearing at his shirt, pushing it away so that the rasping hair of his chest met her naked breasts, and he was kissing her again and taking the inside of her lips with his teeth in urgent response to her own headlong impatience.

She ran her hand down his side, feeling his flesh firm and warm and slicked with perspiration in the hot night. Then her hand was at his belt, tugging it loose, and making him groan.

'Come.' He pulled her over to the mattress, and quickly divested himself of his clothes. When he took her in his arms again he was naked, and for a moment she felt a tremor of fear at her youth and inexperience. She had seen him naked, but not like this, aroused and ready with desire, and, although she longed to touch him, she was uncertain as well. He lifted his lips from hers and looked into her eyes.

'Frankie?'

'I've never done this before.'

'I know.' He took her hand and kissed her fingers, his breath rasping. 'Even now, we don't have to—not if you don't want.'

'I couldn't bear not to. I want you so much. But I'm scared—of disappointing you.'

He read her eyes, then took her hand in his and led her to the heart of his desire. 'There.' He shuddered out the word as her slender hand touched him and knew him. 'Is that what you were frightened of?'

'Not now,' she murmured, marvelling at the firmness which moved in thrusting response to her touch. This was the core of the man who was her lover.

But he stopped her with a tight hand on her wrist and covered her body with his, urgently stroking her breasts and her soft inner thighs until she groaned and reached for him, aching for him to fill her and complete her.

Then he did, and it was like nothing she had ever known before, but a passionate union as they moved together, under the stars, with the sea heedlessly washing the shore below them, and she felt the wonderful symmetry of giving love and receiving it, and whirling astonishment at how far away were the far reaches of desire, where there was no man and woman, no good and bad, no day or night, but just a throbbing, longing, mounting need that possessed her utterly.

'Oh!' She cried out, just as he convulsed against her and she felt his heart hammering in his chest, and an exploding sensation ripped through her and left her shaking.

She opened her eyes, shocked at the violence of her response, and he kissed her instantly, and held her hard and close.

'Don't be startled.'

'I'm not.' It was true. After-waves of delight were washing her body. 'I just didn't know it would be so——' She stopped, seeking the right word.

Cal ran a sensuous hand down her body from breast to thigh. 'So what? So sudden? It isn't always, but we've been in a hothouse together for so long, it couldn't have been any other way——'

She looked at him, her lover, lying against her, and pulled a small face.

'You know so much more about it than me.'

'I'm thirty-two. It would be unnatural if it were otherwise.'

'I know, but I'm jealous of your other women.'

'There isn't anyone else now,' he said firmly. 'Right here and now you're the only woman in the universe I want to be with, and to hold in my arms.' He kissed her deeply. 'And the way I feel now, I could make love to you over and over until morning——'

Luxuriously she kissed him back, inhaling the smell of his skin, and letting her hand caress the muscled strength of him.

'Good, because that's all I want,' she breathed. 'I don't want anything else in the whole world.'

CHAPTER TWELVE

DAWN was showing palely over the sea before they finally slept, their limbs tangled together in sated abandon. When Frankie woke the sun was hot on her skin, and Cal was smoothing her side with a feather-light caress.

'You are perfect,' he marvelled. 'Completely flaw-less.' His hand stroked one shoulder and cupped her breast. 'How do you manage to be so slender, yet to have such wonderful curves, both at the same time?'

Her body stirred for him. She was still awash with the sensations of their night of love, wanting more. She elbowed herself up and looked down at him, her hair brushing across his face. She felt she could feast her eyes for hours on the way his brown, muscled flesh was put together. Her eyes glowed at the sight of him, her lover, the man she loved, and she bent her head to brush her lips to his in a long, dragging kiss.

Cal groaned and reached up for her.

'What on earth did they teach you at that convent of yours?'

She smiled. 'Certainly nothing like this,' she replied primly, moving closer. 'It was mainly geography and etiquette.'

He lay back, and she delighted in touching and stroking his body until he shuddered in delight. She felt wanton and free, in love with every atom of him.

'Oh——' He exhaled a ragged sigh as she leaned

forward and let her teeth tease the sensitive lobe of his ear. 'Then you must be a very quick learner.'

'I had a first-class teacher,' she breathed against his neck, 'and my motivation was excellent. . .'

She ran her hands luxuriously over his chest, glinting a wicked glance at him as she felt his flesh stir more urgently against her.

'Please, Frankie!'

'Please, Frankie, yes? Or please, Frankie, no?'

She felt drunk with delight at the pleasure they found in each other, and moved sinuously against him until he took her hips and, lifting her over him, joined her body to his once more.

Then there was only the exquisite, climbing sensation of delight that she was getting to know so well, and knew she would never tire of. They were lost in each other again, reaching out for the limits of each other's passion until, shuddering with delight, they collapsed together, panting, on their sun-heated bed.

After a long moment Cal turned his head sideways and looked at her. She met his gaze, knowing her love showed in her eyes and not bothering to hide it from him, but when he read her expression he looked away, up at the sun climbing steadily in the sky.

'It must be almost midday,' he said, carelessly. 'I'm so hungry I could eat a horse.'

His words sent a pang of disappointment through her. But what had she expected? Words of endearment? Words of love? Of course not, not when this was nothing more than a passing fling for him.

'We forgot to eat last night.'

He turned his head and looked at her, dark and

fierce. 'We forgot everything. All my good intentions just went out of the window.'

'I'm glad they did. I wanted you so badly.'

'As I did you—and to hell with the consequences.'

'What do you mean?'

'Well, for one thing we forgot to take any sensible precautions. I think I'd better drive into Mombasa this morning.'

She looked at him. Supposing he had made her pregnant? She felt no dismay. In fact, her heart brimmed at the thought of a tiny, dark-eyed baby of Cal's. It would be a part of him to have and to hold forever. But she lowered her head hastily, scared that he would read her thoughts and despise her naked need for him.

'Anyway, I need to check my mail,' he went on. 'I ought to have heard from Elaine by now.'

'Why? I thought you were on holiday.'

'I still need to know where I'm expected to be next.'

She frowned, and he sighed, then reached out a hand to stroke back her hair. 'You know what my life is like. I spend it on planes and trains. There isn't much continuity.'

'I know all that! You don't need to spell it out.' A coldness was spreading inside her like a sheet of ice. 'I'm not getting any false ideas, if that's what you're worrying about. I know this is only a passing affair.' Passing affair. The words went through her like knives, but she hid how she felt behind a defiant, open glance. 'And that's fine by me,' she added bravely, trying to wish the words true. 'I don't want to tie myself down any more than you do.'

He looked at her blackly for a moment. Then he

bent his head and kissed her roughly. 'I've learnt to live in the present, Frankie. And if that's all we've got, then let's for heaven's sake make the most of it.'

So she did, that night and the next, sating herself with the sight and smell and touch of him. Resolutely she blocked out all thought, and gave herself up to the moment, relishing each second they had together. They spent the days fishing and beachcombing, and the evenings drinking wine and talking, and then at night they turned into each other's arms, headlong with need, or sultry with desire.

Cal taught her the moods of love, and she marvelled that there could be so many. They were alone in their tropical paradise, seeing no one, talking to no one. She knew it could not last, but at the same time it seemed it would go on forever.

Every morning they swam, naked as Adam and Eve in the Garden, and once they made love on the wide, empty beach; but it was not a success. The sand seemed to get everywhere.

'I think this only works in films,' she grumbled.

Cal laughed, a deep, rich sound. She propped herself up and looked across at him. His tan had deepened in the sun and his eyes were no longer steely grey, but warmed with blue. Smile lines fanned out from their corners, and his mouth was curved with pleasure. He could have been a different man from the cold, hard figure she had first met in that chilly London drawing-room.

'You should laugh more often.'

He lay back, an arm flung across his eyes against the sun.

'It's not that often I'm alone on a tropical beach with a beautiful, naked girl.'

'Have you ever been?'

He turned, catching her wrist. 'Never with one as beautiful as this.'

'But others, all the same?' Something had got into her. She could not seem to stop the jealous probing. She lifted her eyes and met his with a jolt that stirred some deeper, more ancient longing in her than she had known existed. He was her man, the man she loved, and no other woman had any right to him at all!

'Yes. There have been others; but I can tell you this——' he paused, and his eyes seemed to search hers with an intensity she had never seen before '—never one who makes me feel like you do.'

Her heart was hammering fit to burst. She loved him with her heart and with her soul, and although she had nothing in her young life to compare it with, she knew in some fundamental part of her being that she would never love another man as much.

She closed her eyes, half faint with the feelings that racked her. She had thought that loving him and leaving him would be better than not loving him at all. Now she was not sure. Their affair was a death sentence to her. At twenty she had found the only man she wanted. Yet she could never have him—beyond these few days—and for the rest of her life, she knew, she would carry an emptiness inside.

Another emptiness, she thought bleakly, feeling again the aching hollow where her mother and father had been, and suddenly a tear welled and spilled under her closed lashes.

'Frankie?' She heard a roughness in his voice, then felt his fingers brush away the tear. 'Don't.'

He did not ask her why she was crying. He must have read the anguish in her look and guessed the rest.

There was a long silence, broken only by the sound of the sea. Then he said painfully, 'What we have now is good—it wouldn't always be like this.'

'Why not? Why are you so adamant everything always has to end?'

'Because it always does!'

He abruptly stood up and walked a few paces off, and when he turned back his face was shuttered and stern. He stood before her like a bronzed god on the sand, sunlight glinting on the dark hairs of his chest, but his voice was harsh. 'There are things about me you don't know, Frankie. Things that if you did——' he shrugged cruelly '—would change all this at a stroke.'

She jumped up. 'There isn't anything that would ever change how I feel about you!'

'I wouldn't be so sure; "ever" is a very long time.'

Something had changed. He had withdrawn from her. She could see it in the angry, careless way he bent and picked up his towel, and knotted it around his hips.

'You've still got a lot to learn—about yourself, and about the world.'

'So you keep telling me!'

Bleakly she followed his example and wound her sarong around herself, covering her nakedness.

'One day you'll know I'm right.'

'When it happens, I'll write and let you know.' Her voice twisted with unshed tears.

'Frankie!' He caught her arm hard, whirling her round to face him. 'I never wanted this to happen! God help me, the last thing in the world I wanted to do was to hurt you!'

She was like wood in his grasp. 'You never pretended to me,' she said stiffly, 'and I'm sure I'll get over it.'

His eyes searched hers, harsh and black. 'You've got your life to live, your talents to develop——'

'I don't see why I can't carry on working as your assistant,' she burst out desperately. 'It would help me to learn my craft——'

'No, not any more. That's over now.'

'Another thing that's over! Like everything in your life!'

'Apart from anything else, my shoulder's better. I can do my own driving.'

'I wasn't asking for *your* sake!'

'I know. But it's time for you to make your own way in the world, live your own life. God knows,' he added vehemently, 'you don't want to live mine! No one should live mine!'

'Then why do you do it?'

'I have to. There's a job to be done, and I happen to be the best at doing it.'

'And when will it be finished?' she cried, anguished. 'Never! The wars will go on, and the floods and the famines, and you'll just use yourself up, wear yourself out. You should have seen how you looked back in London. Tired and strained and bitter; I thought you were the grimmest person I'd ever met.'

'Anyone would be grim, seeing the things I see!' He turned sharply from her, as if he was excising her from his life for ever. Frankie could not bear it. 'Cal!' She caught at his elbow, pulling him round, but he only removed her hand as if it were a bothersome insect.

'Leave it, Frankie,' he commanded, and began to walk towards the house, leaving her cold and shivering on the sand at the sudden bitterness which had intruded into their heat-drugged paradise.

She walked away alone along the beach until she was exhausted, then sat in the shade of the palm tree and rested her chin wretchedly on her knees.

Of course she had always known that what they had could not last. But how could she have had any idea how hopelessly she would fall in love with him, how unbearable would be the thought of parting? And if she had known about this pain, would she have fallen into bed with him so eagerly?

Yes, she decided, without hesitation. The last few days had been so perfect that they were worth a lifetime of loss. And anyway, she felt in some way sure that it had been written in the stars, predestined, preordained from the very first moment they had set eyes on each other.

She could remember the moment, just a few weeks ago, when she had knocked so hesitantly on his door in London, but it seemed like a memory from long ago. Then she had been just an overgrown teenager, awash with undirected longings and unhappy frustration. Now she felt years older.

Out here in Africa she had come to know herself more clearly. It was not only that Cal had awakened her body with his, taking her into her womanhood with unerring passion and care—although that had certainly changed her. She moved differently, felt different, and saw a new maturity and depth when she met her own gaze in the mirror.

No, with Cal, on this trip, she had finally found her talents and abilities. Aunt Jenny, bless her, had done her best, but she had always been trying to force a round peg into a square hole. To her aunt, her boldness of spirit, her tomboyish practicality, had been qualities to be muted and hidden. Maybe she had even feared them, seeing too much of her brother in her wayward niece, and dreading she would turn out as feckless and footloose as her father?

But Cal had shown her that he valued them, shown her that she could be herself and follow her own path. And into her empty hands he had put a camera, and with it a future full of possibilities. If she was really as good as he had suggested, then she had a craft to learn, and an art to follow, and after that, who knew what might happen?

For a moment her eyes glowed, then her spirits sank down again. For without Cal none of it would be worth anything at all. Because she knew as clearly as she knew anything that for the rest of her life she would yearn and ache for him as desperately as she did now, sitting forlorn on this deserted, tropical beach.

It was late by the time she walked back, and he was coming to meet her along the shore, a shape materialising out of the distance. She looked at him as they walked nearer, loving the strength of his strong legs, the deepness of his chest, his hair and eyes and face. Then they were close, and he held her elbows and kissed her. His eyes, like hers, were shadowed, but he only said, 'I was worried. You were gone so long.'

'I knew you were busy. I didn't want to distract you.'

He kissed her eyes and throat, dragging his lips lightly across her warm skin. 'Which you would have done. You always do.'

She raised her face to his kisses like a bird feeling spring rain, and breathed in the heady, familiar scent of his nearness.

I love you, she thought yearningly, but beneath his mouth her voice was silent, and only through her kiss did she let her feelings show.

He groaned. 'I want to take you to bed again. Right now.'

'Cal?'

He looked at her.

'You don't regret it, do you?'

'What?'

'Doing what you vowed you wouldn't.'

There was a long silence.

'It would have taken a stronger man than me to resist you,' he said eventually, 'and I'd say you were well ready for it.'

'I was. But only with the right man.'

'Right?' His voice was tight. 'I don't know about that.'

'Well, I do.' She turned to him. 'Whatever happens now, I'll never regret these days together.'

His arms tightened around her, and he looked down into her face. 'I can only pray that that always stays true.'

They walked in silence up to the house. He cast a professional eye at the sun, then said quickly. 'Stay there.'

He went into the house and came out with his

camera, clicking the shutter before she realised what was happening.

'Hey, no!' she protested, backing away, arms up. 'I look a sight.'

'You look lovely. You always look lovely,' he said as he followed her retreating figure, remorselessly clicking.

As she hastened backwards her sarong came loose and fell away. She bent and snatched it up, hearing the relentless clicking of the shuter as she turned and clutched it before her in a pathetic attempt to retrieve her dignity. Giggling and laughing she looked into the lens and in quick-fire succession Cal finished the film.

'You might have let me brush my hair,' she grumbled, rewinding her sarong, but he only laughed.

'Wait.' She ran into the house and came back brandishing the camera he had given her. 'Revenge!'

He looked up, startled, and before he could move she had snapped him several times.

'I loathe having my photograph taken.'

'Is that why you always look so mean and moody in your pictures? I've got a friend who says you look smouldering. I told her it was glowering.' He smiled and she snapped him again, white teeth against brown skin and a fan of smile-lines. 'I suppose it would ruin your image to look happy.'

'I don't have an image,' he said, walking up the veranda steps.

'You do for me,' she said.

'Oh? And what's that?' He turned, waiting for her, and her heart thumped at the sight of him. She laid her camera aside, and walked up the steps to him. Her eyes glinted as she put her hands on his bare chest.

'It's a little too explicit for public consumption.'

His arms went round her and his hands drew her hips to his. 'Ah, that sort of image.' His brooding, sensual mouth set her pulses racing.

'Kiss me,' she said urgently, and he did, fiercely and possessively, until the feelings he aroused in her blotted out her sadness and loss, and there were only the two of them together, and there were very few words, and no coherent thoughts, until they had slaked each other's passion several times over, and the pale tropical moon had risen, turning their abandoned figures into glimmering ghosts in the darkness.

CHAPTER THIRTEEN

IT WAS a night she would remember for the rest of her days—a private time of deep, intense passion, heightened by the knowledge of impending loss—and sleep, when it came, was light and broken.

She got up early, leaving Cal, and went to shower. Then she started to prepare breakfast, slicing papaws and squeezing lemons, but the sound of a bicycle bell startled her, and she left what she was doing to step outside.

Along the narrow, rutted track a man was weaving on a bicycle, ringing his bell to attract her attention.

She waited.

'Telegram for you. No, two telegrams.'

'Two! My goodness! Thank you very much.'

She wiped her hands and took them. One was for her and one for Cal. She went back in frowning.

'What's the matter?' Cal emerged damp from the shower, a towel around his hips.

'The real world's caught up with us at last,' she said harshly.

He flashed her a glance. 'It had to happen some time.'

'I know! That doesn't mean I want it! Oh!' Impatiently she ripped at her envelope.

Photos first-class. Plan picture spread. Need caption information. Please contact soonest. MacArthur. Pictures editor. *Sunday Globe*.

158

She showed Cal. 'They want my pictures.'

He smiled. 'That's terrific! The jackpot first time!'

'I know.' Somehow she could not even smile. Her eyes went to his brown envelope. 'What's in yours?' He took it and went out on to the veranda to read it. It was a long time before he came back, and when he did his face was closed.

'Bad news?'

He shook his head. 'It's my marching orders. The *Sunday Observer* wants to send me back into the lion's den.'

'You mean go after the poachers again?'

He nodded. 'They want the full story. They want me to liaise with the anti-poaching unit and be there when they go in after them. We spoke about it the other day, when I phoned them from John's studio.' He tapped the paper. 'Now they've decided.'

Her heart leapt up. 'Then you'll need me to do your driving!'

'No,' he rapped out. 'I wouldn't dream of it. It's far too dangerous! Anyway, they're sending someone out to work with me.'

'A reporter?'

'That's right.'

'So he'll do the driving.' Her brief elation had gone, casting her down into the pit.

'She'll.'

'A woman!'

'That's right. She's arriving late today.' His expression had become stern and unforgiving. 'This looks like the end of the road for us, Frankie. You'd better catch the afternoon flight up to Nairobi.'

She felt a red, sick, raging jealousy. She could not

bear the thought of his setting off into the bush with another woman. She glared at him, but he had become as grim and remote as the man she had first met in London.

'One in, one out! A right little production line!'

'Don't be foolish. This is just work.'

'But I have to be tidied away before she arrives!'

'Frankie, don't!' he commanded curtly. 'Don't demean yourself. It's been wonderful, but everything comes to an end, eventually.'

'There are endings and endings.' She was hurt more than she could say, wounded by the one blow she had not prepared herself for. This was *their* house, *their* private paradise. Now he was dismissing her so that another woman could come and share his days.

'I agree. Let's try and be civilised about ours.'

'Civilised!' She had never felt less civilised in her life. She wanted to scream and howl with pain. Instead she said tightly, 'I'll go and pack my things.'

Mechanically she folded clothes and collected together her few books. Most of her things, she suddenly remembered, were still at the hotel in Nairobi, but she felt too broken to care.

A girl reporter. She could guess the type. Pushy, self-confident, no doubt with wall-to-wall shoulder-pads and a long line of lovers behind her. The image made her feel very young and insubstantial, and suddenly the thought of home, of her own narrow bed in her own room in Yorkshire, seemed more enticing than anything that was left for her here.

She walked forlornly out of her room. Cal had gone down to the sea, but his telegram lay discarded on the table. She picked it up, and her eyes widened in shock as she read it.

> Darling! My lucky day. Assigned poaching story. Arriving Mombasa Thursday 5 p.m. Expect days—and nights—of fun. Remember Islamabad? All love and kisses. Tania.

There was a noise behind her. She turned. 'And just what happened in Islamabad?'

'It's only a joke.'

Her eyes stripped across his. Her heart was a raw, beating muscle of pain.

'You've been her lover!'

'There's no point exhuming the past.'

'That means yes.'

'All right! Yes! Now are you satisfied?'

'And will be again!'

'Leave it, Frankie! Every affair has its ending and—Tania or no Tania—everything tells me this is ours.'

'Well, she seems to think so, at any rate!' she drove on, waving the telegram in the air.

He shot her a scathing glance. 'Even if she does, these things take two—as I shouldn't have to remind you.'

She shut her eyes, remembering how the full tropical moon hung over the beautiful plains of Africa. Surely he would find it hard to resist such an available offer? Especially knowing what she knew now about his physical needs and vigour. And why should he, anyway? She would be back in London, just another name from his past. Her eyes filled with tears, but she did not want him to see her pain, so she whirled away from him.

'You'll be OK, Frankie. You're tougher than you know.'

'Am I? Well, thanks for the information. I'm sure it'll come in handy some time.'

He drove her in silence to the airport and booked her onward flight to London. He also telephoned the hotel and arranged for her suitcase to be delivered to the airport. She sat motionless, a bundle of hating misery, until her flight was called.

'I suppose I can't even kiss you goodbye?' he said.

She shut her eyes, but he took her in his arms anyway, and she felt the warmth of his arms, the familiar press of his lips. She pushed him away.

'Go and find Tania. She's probably panting with impatience!'

'Vulgarity doesn't suit you,' he said sharply.

'Neither does rejection.' She picked up her bag and began to walk towards the door.

'Frankie——'

She looked back, over her shoulder. He was standing motionless. Their eyes met, but there was nothing they could say. 'Goodbye,' he said. And she turned and walked on, and it was over.

Although many people would have said it was the beginning, not least her friend Alice, who declared she had come back from Africa looking totally wonderful and completely changed.

'That Cal Fenton must have something about him,' she had fished.

'He does. A heart of ice and a skin like leather! The only good thing he did for me was to put a camera in my hand,' she said.

Aunt Jenny was touchingly pleased to see her, when she arrived back in Yorkshire. 'I was worried sick,' she confessed, 'thinking about you out there alone in the bush with that man.'

'Don't worry, Aunt,' she told her. 'I'm tougher than I look.'

She rang the *Sunday Globe* and talked at length about the photo-spread of her work they were planning. 'I think you should come and see me. I think you could probably do some more work for us,' said Doug MacArthur.

'I'm in Yorkshire,' she said dully. She knew she ought to be jumping round the room in excitement, but she felt half dead with misery, killed by the aching hurt she carried inside.

'Get a train,' he said, with evident impatience. 'That's if you really want to be a career photographer. If you're only interested in taking holiday snapshots, forget it.'

'I'll be there,' she said, finally stung into action by his curtness.

And that was how it started. The *Sunday Globe* offered her another assignment, which she took, but completed only with the greatest difficulty. She had longed for Cal constantly on a personal level, now she yearned for his professional help and advice as well.

'It's no good,' she told Doug, after her second attempt at the job. 'I know what I'm trying to do, but I haven't got the skills to achieve it. I need a proper grounding in photography.'

'You're right. You need to work with a professional. Cal Fenton, someone like that. You know him, don't you?' Doug shuffled impatiently among the spilling papers on his chaotic desk. 'Shall I see what I can fix up for you? All these photographers use assistants from time to time.'

'No!' She started up, her response so sharp that Doug stared at her in astonishment.

'He's good,' he said mildly. 'He's the best. Just look at this——' From beneath a tottering pile of photographs he pulled a copy of the *Sunday Observer*. 'Tomorrow's paper,' he explained. 'Someone brought in an early edition.'

Her eyes ripped over the front page and Cal's picture leapt out at her. He was leaning against the Land Rover, his eyes narrowed against the sun, his hair blown by the breeze, his expression enigmatic. How could she have forgotten how unbearably handsome he was? Her heart seemed to leap into her throat. Standing close beside him was a glamorous, dark-haired girl in trousers and a safari-shirt, with a triumphant expression on her face. Jealousy rose up like a red mist before her eyes, fogging the print beneath their picture. 'Stopping the carnage at last. . .latest triumph for *Sunday Observer's* prize-winning team. . .major poaching-gang rounded up. . .considerable personal danger. . .praise from the country's Environment Minister. . .'

Doug turned the page impatiently. 'Oh, that's just the usual stuff. But just look at these pictures—aren't they something?'

He was right. And that something was both graphically sickening and electrically triumphant. Cal had not flinched from shooting the gang's handiwork in nauseating detail, nor had he missed a beat of the way they had been stalked and challenged and captured. In the final photograph one poacher lay sprawled shot on the ground; the rest were penned dejectedly in the back of a decrepit lorry whose contours she could remember in every vivid detail. And as she stared at the pictures, the essence of Africa, and of the man she loved, seemed to leap out at her, to overwhelm her senses yet again in an aching flood of loss.

'They are,' she got out tightly. 'Is the story as good?'

'Oh, Tania's a tough reporter. They make a great team.'

'I see.'

She turned away, frightened that her raging jealousy might show in her eyes.

'So,' Doug leaned back, looking up at her. 'Why don't you want to work with someone like that? It's the quickest way I know of mastering the job.'

'Let's just say I know Cal Fenton well enough to know I could never work with him. He's too arrogant,' she said tensely. 'Anyway,' she added quickly, 'what I really want to do is a proper college course. There's a good one in West London that I've heard about.'

'OK, do it your way.' Doug nodded. 'I'll give you a reference. That should make sure you'll get a place. But how will you afford it?'

'My father left me some money.' She looked up. 'Mike O'Shea. You might remember him?'

Doug nodded slowly. 'I did wonder. It explains a lot about your eye for detail. He was a great correspondent. You should be proud of him.'

'I am, and now I'd like to do something that would have made him proud of me,' she replied, hefting her camera-case on to her shoulder. 'I'll come back to you when I feel I'm ready to start working properly, if that's OK?'

'Do,' he said. 'I look forward to seeing how you turn out.'

Her weeks at college turned out to be both the shortest and the longest of her life. The days and evenings when she absorbed herself in work seemed to fly by. She loved what she was learning, and was delighted to discover a real flair for her chosen profession. Yet at night, when thoughts of Cal crowded her head, the dark hours seemed endless and filled with misery. She heard nothing from him, and did not expect to. She was sure he must have virtually forgotten her existence, especially as his work was appearing from every corner of the world, as if he was travelling ceaselessly and working himself into the ground.

Neither, she lectured herself firmly, did she want to. Someone who could treat her like that, who was so cold and utterly uncaring, was better out of her life forever. But every night, before she slept, she held the photograph of him that she had snapped in the garden of the beach-house, and looked into his darkly smiling eyes, and ached with emptiness inside.

When the course was finished, she took her portfolio along to the *Sunday Globe*. Doug grunted in appreciation, then looked up. 'It's good. I like it. Would you like to do a job for us in Egypt? We've got a writer going out to cover some new excavations in the far south. It'll be rough travelling. No home comforts.'

She thought quickly. Maybe on boats and planes and trains she would manage to forget Cal, just as he had clearly managed to forget all about her. 'I'd love to.'

Doug grunted again. 'Good. I'll get some details

together, but not now.' He checked his watch. 'God, is it that time already? I've got to go. I promised I'd get to Fenton's opening tonight.'

Her eyes widened and her heart leapt and banged at the shock of the familiar name. More than six months had gone by since she had last seen him, but it seemed like yesterday, and her mouth was suddenly dry at the knowledge that he was here, in London, close at hand.

He paused as he shrugged on his jacket. 'Why don't you come? Might learn something. He's the best there is.'

'I know.' She swallowed. 'What's he opening?'

'Not him. He's got an exhibition on at the Photographer's Gallery. It opens tomorrow. There's wine and what-not tonight, but it's practically over. I'll have to put my skates on——'

She had a split second to decide. She ought to say no, of course she should, but instead she found herself saying, 'I'd love to', and then they were down the stairs and in a taxi before she could change her mind.

She was as tense as a bow-string as she walked through the door, but she soon realised that in the crush she would never know if Cal was there or not, and rather than peer nervously through the throng, she detached herself from Doug, and began to tour the exhibition.

All Cal's usual haunting, powerful images were there, and now, as a professional photographer herself, she could appreciate their technical skill as well as their emotional content. Even so, she moved rapidly, desperately wishing that she had not come. She knew Cal must be somewhere in the room, and she wanted to get away, unscathed, as quickly as she could.

But there were two sections at the end which stopped her in her tracks. One was called 'colleagues', and showed half a dozen pictures of television crews working under fire, or journalists besieging famous faces. And there, in the middle, laughing out of a picture of a group of men around a café table, was her father, his eyes merry, his glass raised to the camera. An ache of love and loss seared through her as she saw his familiar features, frozen in time, and she knew from the surroundings that the picture had been taken in Beirut, and that he must have been toasting one of his last days on this earth.

She moved on hastily, tears blurring her vision, and stood blinking before the last two pictures in the exhibition. It was a moment before she could read their joint title, 'Two women in Mombasa'. Then she looked up sharply and confronted her own laughing features, looking with shyness and mischief towards the camera as she caught her fallen sarong up to her shoulders.

The shock held her throat in a vice, flooding her with sensual memories. And the sensuality was there in the picture, too, which hinted at her nakedness behind the thin cotton, and showed the texture of her skin and the intimacy of her relationship with the person behind the lens.

She looked round sharply, but no one seemed to have noticed her. They were all too busy talking and swigging wine. She looked back. 'Two women. . .' the caption said, and there indeed was the other one. Tania. She knew it instantly. Not only did the woman look familiar, from the crumpled newspaper picture that she had smoothed out and peered at so often in the past lonely months, but also it was the same garden, the same palm trees, the same time of year. Although there the similarities ended. This woman lay on an elegant sun-lounger, dressed in a fashionable swimsuit and a wide straw sunhat. A drink and a newspaper lay by her side, and her hand was raised to pull down her sunglasses and look with knowing, lowered lids at the camera.

The two photographs had the impact that was clearly intended. She looked young, carefree and sensual. Tania looked cool, controlled and sophisticated. But, she noticed, the latter also had a perfect figure, dark almond eyes and a firm, even mouth.

Frankie swallowed, the burning sourness of raw jealousy rising in her throat. The sight of the pictures had re-opened all her wounds, until she felt she was raw and bleeding all over.

She turned, looking for the door, but someone was behind her.

'Ah, the mystery revealed at last!' said a drawling female voice. She looked up, straight into the same almond eyes which she had just studied in the photograph.

'Tania.'

'The very same. Mmm. . .' The tall woman looked down at her with a mocking glance. 'I'm afraid I've no idea who you are——'

So Cal had never even mentioned her name. Truly she must have been out of sight and out of mind.

'Francesca O'Shea.' She drew on all the trembling dignity she could muster.

'Well, well,' Tania drawled, 'I must say, I wondered why our Cal took so long to warm up when we were out in Africa together. I decided he must have caught some nasty tropical disease, and didn't like to tell me. But I can see now that his needs had been very well provided for before I even arrived! He probably needed some R & R before he could get going again.'

'I don't know what you're talking about.'

Tania's eyes narrowed, taking in Frankie's glossy curls and green gaze with a jealous stare. 'Come, come. Don't tell me you're a long-lost cousin!'

'I was his assistant. That's all!'

'Darling!' Tania's mocking laugh was so loud that heads turned in their direction all around. 'Anyone can see at a glance what your relationship was with the man with the trigger. Assistants don't walk around with no clothes on, for one thing!'

'You're talking nonsense!'

'Oh, why bother to deny it? After all, we're both in the same boat.'

'Excuse me. I have to go.'

But Tania's eyes held hers. 'He's a disaster for women, you know, an absolute disaster. I've known him for years. Take my word for it. The only thing Cal Fenton loves with any passion is his work. The rest he just——' she shrugged '—snatches on the hoof as it passes by.'

'I'm sure that's very true. But it's of no relevance to me whatsoever. Now, if you don't mind——' Frankie pushed past the woman, heading blindly for the door, only to be stopped abruptly by a pair of hands whose feel she remembered so well that time dissolved and she was immediately back at the beach-house again. Her head reared up.

'Get your hands off me!'

He let her go, and she went straight on past him, not

even looking at his face, out into the night where a light rain cooled her face and masked the shaky tears that brimmed in her eyes. Immediately she began to walk as fast as she could, away down the street.

Then there were running footsteps, and Cal caught her and whirled her round.

'Wait!'

'Let me go.' She shook him off forcefully.

'Why did you come here tonight, if you didn't want to see me?'

'I came with Doug. There wasn't time to think it through properly. If I had, I wouldn't have come near!'

'Doug,' he snorted. 'That sounds very pally.'

She looked up at him, taking in the sight of him properly for the first time. He wore his familiar black leather jacket, with a fresh white shirt. He was every bit as handsome as she remembered, if not more. She longed to lay her head against his chest and be held in his arms forever. Then she remembered Tania, and her gaze hardened on his. 'It isn't, as a matter of fact. I simply happened to be in his office when he was leaving. But what would it matter to you if I was?'

He ignored the question, stripping his gaze over her. 'You look different.' She saw him take in her fashionably tailored suit, the combs that caught her hair back from her face, and the way that work and grief had hollowed away the last vestiges of girlhood from her cheeks. His eyes seem to burn into her.

'Of course I do. I'm older—and a great deal wiser!'

'What are you doing now?'

'I can't believe you care!'

'Oh, I care all right!'

'You have very funny ways of showing it!'

'Maybe I do!'

They glared at each other, chests heaving, antagonism flooding between them. Nothing had changed, she realised, since they had last stood together at Mombasa Airport, nothing at all. Although he certainly looked more strained and tired. A pang went through her, but she forced herself to push it down.

'I've just finished a photography course. I'm hoping to start work now.'

'I could help you——'

'You must be crazy!'

Cal raked his hands through his hair, eyes glittering. 'Suppose there was something I wanted to give you?'

'You've given me enough already, thank you!'

His eyes narrowed. 'What do you mean?' His gaze darted instinctively to her slender waist.

She laughed harshly. 'Oh, don't worry. The gods were on your side. You didn't make me pregnant. That was something, at least, to be thankful for!'

She saw him register her bitterness, and she cringed inside at the harsh sound of her hating voice.

'What, then?'

She tossed her head. Pain. Emptiness. Loss. 'It doesn't matter.'

'Wait there!' He vanished into the night, leaving her alone on the dark street. Then he was striding back, a brown paper packet in his hand.

'I want you to have this. It's a picture. From the exhibition.'

'If it's that picture of me, you can keep it! I'm trying to forget all that ever happened.'

'It isn't,' he said simply, pushing it into her arms. 'You can open it when you get home.'

She looked at him doubtfully, eyes wide, and he stepped towards her, taking her shoulders and saying intently, 'I don't suppose you'll believe me, but I've thought about you so much, wondered where you were, what you were doing, whether you were happy——'

'Happy,' she scorned. She had not been truly happy since the last night she had spent with Cal. 'No,' she said rawly, 'I haven't been happy. How about you? Have you been happy—with Tania?'

'Tania——' He dismissed her with a cut of his hand. Darkness crossed his face. 'Frankie—what happened—it had to be. Believe me.'

'I don't.'

'It couldn't go on like that, don't you see?'

'No, I don't see. I didn't see then, and I don't see now! All I see is an unbelievably arrogant man who casts off one woman for another, and then has the temerity to hang us side by side in a public exhibition like game trophies in a baronial hall!'

'I put those photographs there because they are two of my favourite pictures,' he bit out. 'It would have been less than honest to leave them out.'

'Honest! I don't suppose for a moment you thought what we might feel like——'

'I didn't expect you to come within a million miles of this gallery. I assumed after you left Mombasa you'd never want to see me again. When I saw you here tonight I could scarcely believe my eyes!'

'You mean, that's what you hoped: a pleasant little dalliance, and then a nice clean break!'

'Don't demean yourself, or me. It wasn't like that, and you know it. I'll remind you that there was only one of us that tried to put a brake on what was happening, and it wasn't you.'

Frankie flushed fiercely in the darkness. 'Oh, I threw myself at you! Is that it? Is that your excuse? You didn't stand a chance against my feminine wiles! You were seduced against your will.' Her voice rose, hysterical and bitter with pain.

Cal grabbed her wrist hard. 'I don't need any excuse. What happened between us was one of the best things that ever happened in my life.' Her eyes opened in shock. 'It just couldn't last. Frankie——' Behind them the door of the gallery opened in a flood of light and laughter, and he looked back distractedly. 'Damn! I'll have to go. I'm supposed to be giving a speech——' His eyes went back to hers. 'We can't talk here, like this. Come back with me. We'll have dinner afterwards.'

Her whole being yearned towards him. She almost accepted. But then she forced herself to remember the cold and ruthless man who had turned to her, that last morning in Mombasa, and told her that her time was up. She hesitated for a long moment, but her voice when it came was steady.

'No,' she said. 'I don't think so. In fact I don't think I'd have dinner with you if you were the last person on earth!' And she stalked away into the darkness, leaving him staring at her retreating back.

CHAPTER FOURTEEN

FRANKIE stalked home through the dark streets with rain and tears mingling on her cheeks, and anger raging round her heart. Why on earth had she been so foolish as to go to that exhibition in the first place?

Without stopping to take off her coat, she ran through to the bedroom and snatched up the photograph that stood by her bed. Cal looked out at her, tanned and smiling, a glint in his eye that was all for her.

But it was a lie! That whole episode had been nothing but a sordid little affair, over almost before it started. Only her lurid imagination had built it up into anything more! While she had mooned, lovesick, in London, Cal had been out in the African wilds with Tania, turning to a new woman just as soon as the memory of the last one began to fade.

She hesitated, holding the frame, looking at the picture. She had told herself that this was the real Cal, the warm, true human being beneath the cynical, womanising mask that he wore for the outside world. Yet she had been deluded.

She wrenched the back off the frame and pulled out the photograph. Well, it was really over now. Finished and over forever. And with decisive strength she ripped the glossy print into halves, then quarters, then eighths.

An impatient burst of the doorbell stopped her in

her tracks. She threw the scraps of paper across the bed, and flung open the door.

'Yes?'

Cal shouldered his way in.

'What about your speech?'

'To hell with the speech!'

'What do you think you're doing?'

'Coming in. I don't think there's much point in waiting to be invited.'

'You're right—I want you to go! Right now!'

'When I've said what I've come to say.'

His hair was soaked with rain, and his chest heaved as if he had been running. Carelessly he shrugged off his jacket and threw it across a chair.

Frankie marched across and picked it up again.

'I can't think you've got anything to say that I want to hear!'

She held it out, but he dashed it to the floor with a brutal curse.

'God dammit, Frankie, what's got into you——?'

'Got into me! I'll tell you what's got into me! Tania, for one thing, and the way you hung us both up there in your exhibition like prize trophies! I don't know why you don't go the whole hog and have a wall full of women! And even that wouldn't be all of them, would it? Not with your reputation.'

'My reputation bears very little relationship to the truth,' Cal said crisply, 'and even if it did, I've never tried to hide anything from you! Never pretended to be anything other than I am!'

'I know, I know! I've heard it all before!' She flung her hands up to her ears in exasperation. 'Just like you never pretended we were anything other than a passing affair——'

'That's certainly what it was supposed to be!' he cut in savagely.

'That's what it was! And Tania was the next one.'

'Who told you that?'

She laughed bitterly. 'An impeccable source. The woman herself.'

He cursed again, and turned from her, dashing his fingers through his hair. It was beginning to dry, and she had an absurd, tearing desire to touch her mouth to his neck where it curled damply. In one searing moment she remembered the smell of him, the shape of him, and how his warm skin would feel under her soft lips. Need tore at her guts like a wild animal, but she swamped it with anger.

'I can't say I blame you, or her,' she said bitingly. 'After all, I know what it's like out there—those romantic, moonlit evenings in the bush. I just find it rather hard to take how quickly you moved on——'

Cal snorted harshly. 'As a point of fact there were no romantic, moonlit evenings. We had a rotten trip. Tania got a stomach-bug and was too ill to drive half the time, my shoulder packed up again, and we damn nearly lost sight of the poachers completely. It was only thanks to a stroke of luck, and the tracking skills of one of our rangers, that we managed to pick up their scent again, and even then the whole thing got bungled in the end. No one was supposed to get hurt, but one of our guys turned out to be rather too trigger-happy for my taste. In the end the bullets were flying so fast it was a wonder any of us got out alive.'

Frankie's stomach clenched with deep, instinctive

fear for his safety, but she forced herself to push the feeling away.

'Even so, I dare say it was all worth it in the end!'

'To stop the gang. And to show the world just what poaching really looks like. Yes.' His eyes glinted. 'In fact I've just heard there's to be international action on the issue, thanks to our story.'

'Oh, you're the best. You and Tania, both. Doug told me.' Her voice twisted sarcastically. 'He said you make a great team.'

'We do. When we're working.'

'*And* when you're not—if that glamour-picture in the exhibition is anything to go by.'

'It isn't. If you must know, that was taken after a week of rest and recuperation back at the coast. I was desperate to get out of there, but Tania was in no hurry to leave the beach. She claimed she was too ill to travel. I was practically climbing the walls, snapping everything and anything in sight to pass the time.'

'You could have left without her.'

He snorted. 'You think I didn't think of that? But by then the foreign desk was determined to wring the most out of having us out in Africa together, so they'd ordered us on up to Sudan for a week.'

'How cosy!'

He glinted her a savage glance. 'You've clearly never been to Juba, or you wouldn't say that.'

'At least you were together—without any stomach-bug to get in the way this time.'

'Together—and practically at each other's throats!'

'Yet you still hung her in your exhibition.'

His eyes stripped over hers. 'Yes, I did. To couter-point that picture of you. Don't you see the point?

Tania so posturing, trying to be sexy, and you, so utterly free and natural, yet totally sensual in yourself——'

He stepped towards her. She held her breath at his nearness.

'I don't know what story Tania fed you with tonight, but I'm telling you the truth, Frankie. Nothing happened between us on that trip. Nothing but arguments and irritations!'

Her eyes met his doubtfully.

'Look,' he said in a tone that brooked no interruption, 'Tania and I go back a long way. She's a fine writer and a good colleague. Once, years ago now, we had the briefest of flings. It meant nothing. But what I hadn't realised was that she's always hankered after starting another affair, and she saw this Africa assignment as a perfect opportunity to do so. Until she got ill she tried every which way, and when I wouldn't, as it were, play ball——' his lips quirked a little '—she turned nasty on me. I dare say whatever she said to you tonight was a product of that same bitterness. A woman scorned, and all that.'

Still Frankie looked at him hesitantly.

'What the hell did she say, anyway?'

'Well, to paraphrase her bluntly, she said you were a bit slow to get started, and she realised now it must have been because you'd been getting your oats the week before with me.'

'Slow—oh, my God! There wasn't a woman in the world who could have aroused my ardour after you left! I scarcely felt alive, I missed you so badly!'

'You missed me?' She could hardly believe it.

'More than you'll ever know.'

'Oh, I know all right!'

'I thought about you all the time—where you were, what you were doing, what you were thinking. I worried that you might be pregnant. . .'

She grimaced. 'Not without reason. There was a very long five days when I might have been.' When she remembered those endless days and nights, the agony of her uncertainty and the confusion of her mixed hopes and fears, anger spurted in her again. 'There *are* telephones, you know.'

'Yes, and I spent a lot of time finding them and starting to dial your number, and then putting the phone back again.'

'But why?'

'I knew how angry you were when you left me. And anyway, I knew I had to let you go.'

Suddenly Frankie felt immensely tired. She sank down wearily on a chair. Cal's astonishing declaration had sparked a flowering joy in her, but now his words doused the brief flare.

'Then why are you here now?'

He came and crouched before her. 'Because when I saw you tonight I knew I had to. Seeing you there, looking so beautiful, so utterly yourself, I knew I couldn't bear to let you go again.'

She raised her head to meet his look, and her heart lurched at the sight of him.

'Frankie——' He reached for her hands and began to draw her to him, but he stopped when he saw tears brimming in her eyes.

She tried to gulp them back, but it was too late. Sobs were starting to rack her frame. 'No! I don't want it! I can't do it,' she cried. 'I can't bear the pain of it again.'

His hands moved to her arms, holding her as she shook and cried, and suddenly her words were spilling out without restraint. 'You were right all along. We should never have got involved! I wasn't thinking straight. I just wanted you so badly, I don't know what I thought. I think part of me even believed I could make you love me, make you stay. The other half thought I could cope when it was over, but I couldn't——' Cal still held her, waiting for her breathing to steady, but, with a firmness of spirit that amazed her, she pushed his hands away, stood up, and walked away.

'I don't know why you're here now, Cal, but I do know one thing, and that's that you won't be here tomorrow. You'll be in Afghanistan, or Argentina, or Australia. You certainly won't be here. You've told me often enough what your life is like, and I've finally learned my lesson—the hard way. I don't want another brief affair! And I don't want you walking in and out of my life whenever the fancy takes you!' She whirled and faced him, the tears still coursing down her face. 'And since that seems to be why you're here, you'd better go!'

He met her gaze, dark and level.

'That isn't why I'm here. It's how things should have been, how I intended them to be. But you were different, I knew it right from the first day we met.' He stood up, facing her squarely. 'That's why I was so tough on you, so determined to keep you at arm's length. Then, when I took you to bed, I told myself it was because you were so utterly irresistible and my defences were down. But it wasn't like that at all. I found myself wanting and needing you so much it terrified me——' His eyes met hers. 'Do you understand? I didn't want to feel like that. I didn't want to be tied down to anyone. It had never been part of my plans. So when that telegram came it seemed a good way of saving both our skins.'

'What——?' Frankie's brain turned wildly.

Cal strode over to her and gripped her elbows, almost shaking her. 'Don't you see? I'd always been a loner. I felt there was no place in my life for anything or anybody that threatened to be permanent! And on top of that you were so young, and so vulnerable—I felt it was my duty to push you away before you got too hurt by what had happened. When Tania's telegram came I had only two things on my mind. The first was how to get you out of there as quickly as possible—I knew it was an ugly story they'd put me on, and my priority was to get you well clear of any danger. The second was how I could send you away thinking the worst of me, and that telegram seemed too good a chance to miss.'

Her eyes went to his.

'I know you meant me to read it. That's why you left if lying around, isn't it?'

He shrugged. 'I don't think it was quite that conscious. But I could see you were falling in love with me, and I suppose I wanted to stop the process in its tracks.'

She shook her head. 'Nothing could do that. After I left I missed you so badly I really thought I could die!'

Pain and love snagged in their gazes.

She searched his look. 'Is this what you came to tell me?' she asked him.

'No. I didn't mean to say any of this. At least

not——' He stopped. 'I've come to talk about something much more difficult. About a picture. That picture I gave you tonight.'

She looked around, then remembered it was in the bedroom where she had dropped it on the bed in her earlier blind rage. 'I'll get it.'

He followed her, and his eyes went to the scattered fragments of photograph that lay beside the parcel on her bed. Frankie flushed at the evidence of her earlier violence. He looked at her greyly.

'Is that what you think of me?'

'I was so upset at seeing you again.'

She bent to gather them up, but he said curtly, 'Leave them. In a few moments you may feel just the same. Sit down. This is serious.'

She sat on the bed and undid the wrapping. Mike's face leapt up at her from the photograph, full of life and joy. She smiled into his smile. Cal watched her.

'That picture was taken the night Mike died.'

'Oh!' Her eyes widened in shock.

He began slowly. 'We'd all been out together, celebrating one of the journalists' birthdays. After the meal was over, I said I was going to mooch about a bit, and take some photos. It was a warm night, in a safe part of the city, and I didn't feel much like sleeping. Mike said he wanted to come with me, so we strolled around, and had another drink or two, and then, as we were walking home, I spotted some children playing down a side-street in some bombed-out buildings.'

Frankie flashed a glance to him, and saw how dark his eyes had grown as he followed his memories.

He went on, 'I told Mike to wait while I went down this narrow alley and took some shots, but he followed me down and stood leaning on a car while I worked. When I finished I went across to him and leaned against the car next to his, and then——' his eyes went to hers, holding her look '—I don't fully remember what happened next. All I remember is Mike shouting and pushing me violently backwards so that I fell across the street. Then there was a great roaring sound, and flames and smoke everywhere, and Mike and the car were gone.'

'Oh!' Frankie forgot to breathe as she followed the awfulness of his tale.

'People came running to tend me,' he said. 'I kept shouting at them to help Mike, and I couldn't understand why they wouldn't. Then I realised there was nothing they could do.'

She swallowed.

'To this day I don't know whether Mike saw something, or heard something, or what, but I know he saved my life—and that it cost him his own.'

There was a deep silence in the room. He said rawly, 'Frankie, your father would have been alive today if it wasn't for me. He was only there, in that spot, on that night, because of me. And even then, if he hadn't thought about my life, he might have saved his own.'

She looked at the carpet, lost in thought.

'I loved Mike,' he said hoarsely, 'and I respected him, and he was just gone.'

'It wasn't your fault——' she burst out, but he stopped her with a raised hand.

'Don't. I've rehearsed all the arguments a million times over. About how it could have happened anywhere, and how I didn't put the bomb in that car, and all the rest of it. But all I'm left with at the end of the day is how I feel—and how I feel about it is——' He stopped, wordlessly shaking his head.

Frankie looked at him, not knowing what to say. He met her eyes. 'And, to put it bluntly, deflowering his only daughter didn't make me feel any better.'

'Mike was a realist. If he'd lived to see me grow up, he would have known I had to start living my own life. And you hardly seduced me against my will.'

'Even so——'

'Don't you think he might have been glad it was you?'

'No, I don't. I think he would have wanted someone better for you. Someone who wasn't about to hop on the next plane to Timbuktu.'

'There is no one better for me! Don't ask me how I know it, I just know!' She glared at him, loving him and hating him so much that she thought her heart would break. 'You're better for me, even if you are in Timbuktu!'

Her words drove the worst of the bleakness from his eyes. He looked at her for a long time, and his expression slowly changed until smile-lines softened his eyes.

'I'm not sure there'll be so much Timbuktu from now on,' he said quietly. 'I've done a lot of thinking these past few months, and it seems it might be time to stop catching so many planes and trains.'

Frankie scanned his face, not knowing what he meant.

'When I started to fall in love with you, all I could think of was how much you would despise me when you knew about Mike! And that was another very good reason for sending you packing. I couldn't bear to see the pain in your eyes.'

'Love?' she echoed, wonderingly. She held his look. 'What you just told me isn't a shock to me. I think I knew anyway, or half knew. First of all it was something those drunken journalists in Nairobi said, that night you pretended I was your girlfriend. Then, when you were delirious, and were shouting in your sleep, you said things that made me wonder—but I blocked it all out of my mind. If you didn't want to tell me, I guess I didn't want to know.'

Slowly he reached for her hand, holding it as if it were the most precious object on earth. 'Do you know when I first started to fall in love with you?'

She shook her head, dumb with the happiness that was starting to burgeon inside her.

'I think it was when you came into the hotel in Nairobi and coolly announced you'd changed that Land Rover tyre. Then later, when we were in the bush together, I could hardly think straight because of the way you were at my side all the time in those skimpy T-shirts and provocative shorts. Have you any idea what you look like, crawling backwards out of a thorn brake?'

'Only because you made it so plain you didn't like it.'

'Like it!' He rolled his eyes. 'I had the devil's own job to maintain any sort of decorum.'

'I was frightened of you at first,' she confessed. 'You seemed so cold and hard, and I told myself I didn't like you. But I was attracted to you as well—as you well know.' She blushed. 'Then later, when we were kidnapped, and afterwards, when you were ill, I knew I was falling in love with you. And then I just felt so desperate, thinking you only saw me as some sort of convent schoolgirl.'

'I tried to, I really tried; but it didn't last. You got under my skin in a way no other woman ever has. Sometimes you drove me half crazy with exasperation. Sometimes you told me home truths I certainly didn't want to hear. But all the time I was falling more and more in love with you.' He drew her into his arms. 'I didn't want to take you on the trip, I didn't want to take you to bed, I didn't want to fall in love with you—you've been nothing but trouble since I first set eyes on you!' He was talking against her mouth, her hair, her ear, pulling her closer. 'I might even have made it, except for that drunken young sailor in Mombasa. When I saw him pawing you, I just saw red! That's my woman, I thought! I felt so fiercely possessive I could have killed him on the spot! Even then, though, I tried to kid myself. I thought a quick, torrid affair would get you out of my system.'

'I thought it did!'

'Oh, no! The more I had, the more I wanted of you. Not just your body, but your mind and spirit, too. It was hell to send you away.'

'Oh! So much needless pain!'

He set her back from him to look at her.

'No, not needless. You needed time away from me—to find your own feet and be sure of your own mind. And I needed time to know I had to find you, and time to find the courage to tell you about Mike.'

Frankie pushed closer into his arms. 'Mike would have said, "It's just one of those things", or "The past is the past". He would probably have wanted to knock our heads together. He always said happiness was fleeting and you had to grab the moment.'

'But I want more than a moment,' he said roughly. 'I want all the moments there are. I used to hate the thought of permanence and commitment, but now I couldn't stand to settle for anything less. I want you for always, Frankie, to make you mine.'

'There's nothing I want more.'

He groaned and kissed her deeply. 'How about getting married? Tonight? Tomorrow?'

'I'll have to break the news to Aunt Jenny——'

'Then next week?'

She pulled back, frowning. 'Oh! I've promised to go to Egypt, to do a job for Doug. But I'll cancel——'

'Nonsense. I'll wait for you. Just come back to me, and don't you dare look at any other men while you're there!'

'There aren't any other men, as far as I'm concerned. I'd resigned myself to lifelong celibacy, before tonight!'

Cal kissed her again, long and sensuously, his hands roaming her shoulders. 'You weren't born to be celibate.'

'Or to live without you.' Her hands reached up to hold the broad strength of his shoulders, and they fell back together on the bed.

'Oh, Frankie, my love,' Cal groaned. 'I've ached for this moment. I'll love you in all the ways possible, for the rest of my life. I give you my solemn word.'

And that was quite enough for her, Frankie thought, pulling him down to her again, because there was nothing more solid and steadfast in the whole world, and she lifted her lips with love to feel the sealing joy of his kiss.

WIN A LUXURY CRUISE

TO THE MEDITERRANEAN
AND BLACK SEA

Ever dreamed of lazing away the days on the open sea with all you need to enjoy yourself close at hand, and spending busy, exciting hours ashore exploring romantic old cities and ports?

Imagine gliding across calm blue waters with the sun overhead in a vast blue sky, and waking up in faraway places for breakfast, such as Lisbon with its fashionable shops, or at the famous rock of Gibraltar.

Imagine sailing through the Mediterranean and stopping at Sicily with towering Mt Etna, then arriving effortlessly in Athens with all its many treasures and finally cruising along the Bosphorus and exploring the exotic city of Istanbul.

This experience of a lifetime could be yours, all you need to do is save the red token from the back of this book and collect a blue token from any Mills & Boon Romance featuring the holiday competition in December. Complete the competition entry form and send it in together with the tokens.

Don't miss this opportunity!
Watch out for the Competition
in next month's books

Next month's Romances

Each month, you can choose from a world of variety in romance with Mills & Boon. These are the new titles to look out for next month.

THE STONE PRINCESS Robyn Donald

TWO-FACED WOMAN Roberta Leigh

DIAMOND FIRE Anne Mather

THE GOLDEN GREEK Sally Wentworth

SAFETY IN NUMBERS Sandra Field

LEADER OF THE PACK Catherine George

LOVEABLE KATIE LOVEWELL Emma Goldrick

THE TROUBLE WITH LOVE Jessica Hart

A STRANGER'S TRUST Emma Richmond

HIS WOMAN Jessica Steele

SILVER LADY Mary Lyons

RELUCTANT MISTRESS Natalie Fox

SHADOW HEART Cathy Williams

DEVON'S DESIRE Quinn Wilder

TIRED OF KISSING Annabel Murray

WIFE TO CHARLES Sophie Weston

STARSIGN

STARS IN THEIR EYES Lynn Jacobs

Available from Boots, Martins, John Menzies, W.H. Smith and other paperback stockists.

Also available from Mills and Boon Reader Service, P.O. Box 236, Thornton Road, Croydon, Surrey CR9 3RU.